At first Deborah Fellowes and her Uncle Ronnie think they've caught a poacher but it soon emerges that they're on the trail of someone far more sinister . . .

One spring night, Deborah and her uncle are out looking for foxes when, caught in the glare of their lamp, they see the figure of a trespasser. Elbows whirling and coat flapping the man rushes past them, grabbing at Ronnie's gun and knocking it from his hand. But before he can be identified, the fugitive vaults over a wall and disappears.

The incident sets Ronnie thinking. Was this the man responsible for the discreet poaching discernible in the neighbourhood? The mystery deepens when a shotgun stolen years earlier is found abandoned in the heather.

Deborah's husband Ian, the local CID inspector, begins to investigate. And the results of a fingerprint search done on Ronnie's gun prove extremely surprising. Because the prints belong to a wanted man, on the run after a notorious case of theft and fraud during which two of his colleagues died and the accumulated profits from years of crime vanished in an instant. Are Ronnie and Ian closing in on a ruthless killer on the run from justice?

Carriage of Justice

Gerald Hammond

MACMILLAN

First published 1995 by Macmillan London

a division of Macmillan Publishers Limited
Cavaye Place London SW10 9PG
and Basingstoke

Associated companies throughout the world

ISBN 0-333-63639-2

9 8 7 6 5 4 3 2 1

A CIP catalogue record for this book is available from
the British Library

Phototypeset by Intype, London
Printed by Mackays of Chatham PLC, Chatham, Kent

FOREWORD

It seems that I have been conscripted into the task of editing my uncle's book, translating it from dog-Doric into acceptable English and filling in some details from my own knowledge.

To be frank, this is going to be one hell of a chore. Uncle Ronnie's writing, apart from looking as though it has been executed in treacle with a blunt stick, is to calligraphy what dog-piddle in the snow is to a Rembrandt; and even his use of more or less traditional Scots spelling is misspelled.

Well, at least it will be something to do while I'm waiting for this baby to arrive.

The only other consolation is that, because my uncle's reading is confined to the back pages of the local paper and selected items in the shooting and fishing magazines, he is unlikely ever to set eyes on the finished text. My insertions (in italics) can therefore be as frank as I care to make them. I only ask that any friends who read this book do not draw them to his attention.

Deborah Fellowes

ONE

There's a lot of damned nonsense talked about foxes, mostly by armchair conservationists who've never seen a fox outside a zoo. It's true that the fox is a handsome creature, and intelligent with it. You can respect them. You could even like them if they weren't such bad buggers.

But to say that a fox only eats worms and small rodents, or that it'll only take a lamb that was going to die anyway, that's just daft. Shoot a fox and empty its stomach and you'll be amazed what you'll find, anything from fruit to a kitten. A fox may eat a lot of voles, but it'll not pass up the chance of a nesting bird and if it gets among poultry it won't just take what it needs, it'll kill the whole lot. A hungry fox will tackle a young but hale lamb any day, and in savage weather I've come across a ewe that's had its udder ripped open so that a fox could get at the milk. I've known a fox to bite the head off a lamb while the rest of it was still inside the mother ewe. To top it all, the fox is the main spreader of rabies in Europe.

So I'm no lover of foxes, though I'm always sad when I kill one. I don't blame the fox, mind you. It's in the fox's nature to be as it is and it's in my

3

nature to be against it. When Sir Peter said to get out there and do something about them, I went.

I've worked for Sir Peter Hay, both in Newton Lauder and up north, almost since I left school, which is a good few years now. I'm his stalker and ghillie, supposed to be, but the days have gone by when an estate could carry a full complement of staff, so when he's no keeper or the keeper needs a hand, that's down to me too. The keeper at that time, who was damned good with the gun, couldn't hit a barn from the inside with a rifle; and a rifle's the right weapon for a fox.

Mind you, although fox numbers are higher than ever they were, what with them breeding in the towns, keepers being a dying breed in the countryside and so-called enlightened folk pulling up and carrying off snares whenever they find them, I was fairly sure that we'd no more of them than usual. None of the earths showed signs of being in use, although it was early enough for that, and I'd seen little sign of their droppings. An occasional visitor from the unkeepered land over the boundary, maybe, looking for an easy meal, but no resident foxes.

I said as much to Sir Peter. We were standing at the corner of the track just below the high moor, in a wind that would have made a brass monkey think twice. He's an old man now but a proud one. He will wear the kilt and he feels the cold terribly, but he wouldn't get back into the Land-Rover until he'd had his say.

'What about all the tracks Young Hamish was finding after the last snowfall?' he demanded.

'Young' Hamish was what they called the keeper,

to distinguish him from his father, now retired from the same job.

'That was a dog,' I said.

'A dog fox?'

'A dog dog,' I said. 'Probably Mrs McIndoe's terrier going after the rabbits.'

'But Hamish said it was a fox.'

'He's just a laddie,' I said. 'He doesn't know it all. The toes were too spread for a fox. And a fox walks so that its rear paw lands in the print of the forepaw.'

'Young' Hamish was thirty-five by then and becoming a very good keeper. But I'll admit that he was wrong about the foxes.

'And those sad little piles of feathers we were finding?' (I held my peace. The ground was being poached by somebody who wanted the blame put on foxes, but it was none of my job to tell Sir Peter and land Young Hamish in trouble.) 'Anyway, Jenkins has lost a couple of lambs and he thinks the fox came from here, so we've got to show willing. You'll have a go at them?'

'Of course, Sir Peter,' I said.

'And I'll get onto the Forestry Commission, or whatever they call themselves now, and give them a push. It's a bad-neighbour policy, not controlling foxes until they're asked.' Sir Peter looked at me as though that change of policy was my fault. Then he nodded and got back into the Land-Rover at last, holding out his thin old hands to the windscreen heater. 'And keep an eye on the old dens, Ronnie,' he said. 'But be canny. The slightest sign of trouble and a vixen will move house – and her cubs, when she's got them. An earth that's empty today can be occupied tomorrow.'

That much was true. I'd told him it myself, but he's getting forgetful.

I've nothing against fox-hunting, myself. It must be grand fun following the hounds and at the end of it the fox is either killed, quick and clean, or it gets clear – not wounded as can happen if you take a shotgun to it. And while snares may be working for you while you're asleep I don't relish the thought of the waiting. No, that's not the way to control foxes. The most effective method is with a lamp and a rifle after dark, provided that the rifle's well handled.

There was no point going out that night or the next. We were having a spell of real winter. Where, I wondered, was all the global warming we'd been promised? Not that I mind a bit of hard weather, you understand. I'm in no fear that I'll dissolve. But when there's rain or sleet falling, you look through the telescopic sight and every raindrop or snowflake is glowing like a distant torch in the light of the lamp. Even between showers, you don't shoot well when your fingers are frozen – and a fox that's been shot at and missed will be lamp-shy from them on.

Then, all of a sudden, winter decided that it had gone on long enough for the moment and it looked as though spring might arrive some month soon. The sun came out and there was a warm, dry wind. Small trees which had been bowed down with the weight of snow stood up straight and whole fields which had been frozen like iron first turned to porridge and then became firm again.

Lamping for foxes is best done from the back of a pick-up, which means that you need somebody to drive and maybe work the lamp. (Three's even better with one just to work the lamp and open gates.) It's not everybody that's willing and competent to drive around the dark fields, taking instructions by way of knocks on the roof of the vehicle. But my niece Deborah knows the job and she wasn't doing anything else at the time.

Except for looking after a house and husband and helping my father out at the workbench from time to time. Uncle Ronnie has never accepted that I'm a time-served gunsmith. To him, I'm still about six years old and yet somehow able to drive and shoot.

If I had known that I was pregnant, nothing would have induced me to go bouncing around off-road in his terrible old Land-Rover. At the time, I was putting the cause of my occasional squeamishness down to my sudden craving for banana splits, instead of the other way around.

The first night, we zigzagged around the fields until my legs were shaking from jumping down to open and close gates. Plenty of rabbits were out in the fields, but not a sign of a fox coming after them or after the partridges which had jugged down in the stubble.

Two nights later, we were out again. This time we

followed the boundaries of Sir Peter's land, to see if we couldn't intercept a fox coming in from outside, and damned if the headlamps didn't pick up a fox loping across some open ground between the big wood and some spring barley. Deborah needed no signal from me. She swung the Land-Rover to a halt and held the lamp on him and I shot from the open back of the Land-Rover and bowled him over. Two hundred yards, it must have been, but my treble-two rifle throws a two-inch group at that distance if I'm properly set with my elbows braced on the roof of the cab.

And so it should, the hours I spent lapping the barrel, fitting a micro-bedder and tuning the trigger. And never a word of a thank you, except for a bottle of Highland Dew – to my dad!

The next night but one, we went out again. Not a single fox was to be seen in the fields. Before giving it up, at about three in the morning, I decided to try a place at the corner of the moor where several fox routes meet. Foxes tend to follow the same fixed paths. Even if there's not been a fox on the land for a year, the next one along will nearly always follow the same paths as the last one.

The nearest we could bring the Land-Rover was a hundred yards or more from where I decided to lie in wait. Deborah wanted to stay in its shelter and have a sleep, but I needed her along. I've a lightweight halogen lamp that clips on to the 'scope of the rifle, but I was also taking along a shotgun because sometimes your first sight of a fox is close, the moment the lamp goes on, just before he bolts into cover, and you'll get him with a load of Number Three where you'd surely miss with a single bullet. Lop, my collie, came along. Collies can make good gun dogs, although the nobs look down their noses at them.

'Do you want to handle the lamp or the shotgun?' I asked her.

'The gun,' she said. So I clipped the lamp to the rifle and put the heavy little battery in my pocket. We set off in almost total darkness, following a well-remembered route as quietly as we could, more by the feel of the path than by the faint light that the stars managed to push through the clouds. We climbed a gate the same way and settled down in the best place I knew, sitting on fallen stones with our backs against a dry-stone wall. Lop squeezed between us for warmth. I tried my position and found that I could get a good rest for my elbow on my knee. We couldn't see a thing, but I knew that ahead of us was a fox path and another coming from our left. In daylight we could have seen all the way across the moor to where the ruins of an old castle, little more than tumbled walls and the base of a tower, stood on a hillock.

'No glow tonight,' Deborah said.

'No.' Sometimes a faint glow could be seen above the castle. It was an eerie sight. There were stories told about that castle that would make the hairs prickle up your back. There had been doings there during the fifteenth century, I'm told, and again two hundred years later, that were better not to be thought about. Folk who believe in the supernatural wouldn't go near the castle after dark, not for the promise of a reserved seat in heaven.

And Uncle Ronnie was one of them.

I began to squeak. You can buy a squeaker in the gun shops, but if you suck the back of your hand, as I was doing, you can make the same noise, just like a rabbit that's caught in a snare. If there's a fox within a quarter of a mile, or further on a frosty night when the sound travels, that will fetch him.

We waited, listening. There's no point flashing the lamp too soon and scaring Charlie away. Once or twice I squeaked again, for encouragement. I thought for a moment that I could see the glow over the castle but I knew that it was just the straining of my eyes. You can see whatever you expect to see in the dark and at that hour of the morning. I wished to God that Sir Peter would spring for an image intensifier – their price had dropped dramatically since the Russians started dumping military equipment on the market – but his acceptance of new technology is usually twenty years behind the times.

I heard a sheep go by, sounding like an old man with a nasty cough. Something had disturbed it.

There was a faint sound from somewhere in front of us, about where the grass gave way to heather. Lop stirred and Deborah nudged me. I felt her bring up the gun and heard the faint click of the safety catch. I already had a round in the chamber.

I lined up the rifle with where I thought the sound had come from and pressed the button on the back of the lamp, ready to sweep the beam round the open ground in front of us.

10

Right in the middle of the bright beam and not more than ten yards away was a figure which turned and came rushing at us, all whirling knees and elbows and a flapping coat. He was a lucky man not to be shot dead. It was only that we had ghosts and goblins in our minds that froze us to the spot.

It was over in a moment. He knocked the rifle out of my hands and grabbed at the shotgun as he went by, but Deborah hung on. Lop had to make a leap to avoid being stamped on. The light went out. There was a rattle of stones. He must have vaulted over the wall behind us and he was gone before Lop could even bark and long before Deborah's scream had died away. I felt Lop crouch to leap the wall and go after him but I stopped him with a word. There was no saying where such a chase might end – in front of the sheriff or in the vet's incinerator.

We heard one mad yell out of the darkness and then all was quiet.

We sat where we were for a minute or two, not knowing what had happened and not really believing it. Lop was rumbling quietly to himself for reassurance. 'Who the hell was that?' I said at last, really wanting to know.

'It wasn't any of my friends. How about yours?' she said, the impudent bizzum.

There was no point trying to follow the man up. He was in an area of tall gorse and bracken with occasional tracks made by sheep and deer. Even in daylight a man could vanish totally there. I got out my little pocket torch and examined the rifle. The lamp was a ruin and the 'scope would have to be zeroed again but otherwise it seemed undamaged, which was one mercy. Lamping was surely over for the night, but even if there had been a fox near by he was well warned off. I heard Deborah unload the shotgun.

We set off back towards the Land-Rover. 'He'll never know how near he came to being blown in half,' Deborah said. 'Are you going to tell the police?'

I thought about that. I didn't fancy going to the desk sergeant with a tale about wild men on the moor. There is only one of them who's any use in a poaching matter. 'You could tell your man when you get home,' I said. My niece had married a policeman.

My husband was and is a detective inspector, the pinnacle of CID in Newton Lauder. To my uncle, a policeman is a policeman, be he a traffic cop or the Commissioner of the Met, and as such is to be mistrusted.

'I'll tell him in the morning,' she said. 'If I'm awake before he goes out.' She always was a sleepy-head.

I had a good look round in the morning. Rather than drop Young Hamish into Sir Peter's bad books, I took the keeper out in the morning and showed him some of the signs – a tin can buried to its neck where a grouse, looking for grit, could drop inside and be unable to climb or fly out, a snare set for rabbits deep inside a hedge. At a 'sad little pile of feathers', as Sir Peter had called it, we squatted down and I showed him that the wings had been ripped off rather than chewed and that the feathers were neatly plucked.

'But why didn't you tell me earlier?' he asked me.

'I've been telling you and Sir Peter for months that there was a poacher about,' I told him. 'It wasn't my job to make you look more of a gowk than you are.' The fact of the matter was that, though I despise the organized gangs of poachers who come and slaughter the game and deer or net the rivers for a quick profit, I have some respect for a man who uses real fieldcraft to get away with a bird or two and the occasional rabbit under the keeper's nose, just as long as he leaves the deer alone and respects nesting seasons.

The 'fact of the matter', I suspect, was that my uncle did not want to let on how much he knew about the poaching of game-birds when his field of expertise is supposed to be deer and salmon. According to local legend, in their youth he and my dad were the craftiest pair of poachers for miles around.

So Hamish reported to Sir Peter that he had changed his mind and that there was a poacher around after all. Sir Peter came looking for me and found me hanging a roe carcass in the game larder.

'What's this I hear about you and Deborah surprising a poacher up by the High Moor?' he asked me.

I told him the story and he sighed. 'I suppose I'll have to pay for another lamp,' he said.

While we were on that subject I decided to try him again for that image intensifier. 'That's if you're

13

serious about controlling the foxes and not just wanting to "show willing",' I said.

'I don't see why you want it,' he grumbled. 'You manage very well without.'

'I manage to lamp from a vehicle. Lying in wait, it's a different matter. Switch on the lamp too soon and you've warned him away. If you can watch him until he's just where you want him and well away from cover . . .'

'We'll see,' he said, and I knew that that was an end of the matter for the moment. 'About that man. It wasn't anybody you recognized?'

'He had a fine set of beard and whiskers, like nobody I can think of around here.'

'They could have been false, thought it hardly seems likely.' He gave me a piercing look. His body may be getting frail but his eyes are as sharp as ever. 'So you're sure we don't have any foxes in residence?'

'Just the occasional wanderer,' I told him. 'I'll keep an eye on the old earths in case a vixen moves in.'

'Hamish can do that. I want you to go back up north.'

'We've finished the hind cull,' I reminded him.

'I know that. But there are two American couples coming.'

'There'll be nothing for them. Can Wullie not manage?' I asked.

'They were over for the pheasants but the weather tempted them to stay on. The ladies want to try for a spring-run salmon while you take the men on the hill. I know we've got our planned quota, but another hind or two will be neither here nor there.'

'I'd better see to the ladies,' I said. 'Wullie's no great hand at the fishing.'

'Wullie's getting too old for scrambling around on the hills. Do it the way I said.'

So I spent the next week up at the Dawnapool estate, choosing barren hinds for the Americans to shoot, stopping them from going after trophy stags in the close season and introducing them and their ladies to some of the better highland malts of an evening.

With uncharacteristic modesty, Uncle Ronnie has skipped over Sir Peter's real reason for keeping him away from the river. My uncle was never a beauty but, although he must be nearer fifty than forty, he has kept a sort of rugged masculinity that some women find irresistible. There have been complaints. American visitors do not appreciate a return from the hill to find their wives fishless but tousled and contented and with their delicate cheeks apparently sandpapered by stubble.

I got back to my small house in the late evening, tired after the long drive in the Land-Rover. I had phoned to say that I was coming. There was a note from Sir Peter on the mat to say that Ian, Deborah's husband, would like us both to go and see him in the morning.

Molly, who is my sister and Deborah's mother, had been in and left me a meal in the oven. I had a good dram with it and went to bed and slept like a log. I'm getting a bit old for short nights and long drives in a heavy vehicle.

In the morning, Sir Peter fetched me in one of his

own Land-Rovers – his oldest, but one that's in a far better state than mine. For years I've been hinting that it's maybe time that he passed it on to me and let my one go for spares. One of these days, when somebody's slammed a door too hard and my old banger's disintegrated into a shower of red dust and I'm down to Shanks's pony, he may take the hint.

'The heather's just about right,' he said. 'If this breeze holds we'll start burning tomorrow. Hamish is up there now with the tractor and brush cutter. Deborah's coming. You'll lend a hand?'

'Surely,' I said. There was no need to say any more. Grouse, and all the other moorland creatures, need mixed ages of heather to give them all they need in the way of food and shelter. This is managed by a muirburn – burning the heather in narrow strips on an annual cycle, getting over the whole moor every so many years depending on the quality of the heather. But it has to be done just right, neither hot enough to kill all the seeds nor so mild as to leave dead and decaying matter unburned. This means that a time has to be chosen, between the beginning of October and the middle of April, when the heather's just right. And each fire has to be controlled, which is why the call is for plenty of experienced helpers.

I'm never at my ease, walking into the police building. It's not that I'm guilty of anything, not often, but there's a feeling in the air of suspicion and misery. They say that a building can hold onto the emotions of its occupants and, let's face it, nobody ever went into a police station because they were happy. But Ian was friendly enough when he came to fetch us up to his office, and a civilian clerkess went for coffee from the machine. Deborah was waiting there, looking full of life. (*You could put it like that, I suppose!*) Sir Peter gave her a kiss but there's nothing in that. She's his god-daughter.

When we were all seated and sipping coffee like a hen-party Ian took charge of the talking. He's a square-faced, sandy-haired lad who can sort out a bar brawl in a matter of seconds. (*He is also very handsome and he can comfort a lost child better than most policemen.*) He said, 'Deborah told me about the poacher on the moor. I suppose he really was a poacher and not just some wandering tinker?'

'Not a doubt of it,' I said. 'As he went by, something soft and heavy in his pocket hit my shoulder. A rabbit, I think.'

'I smelled rabbit,' Deborah said. 'Nothing else.'

Ian looked down at the top sheet of one of those long, folded papers with perforated sides that come out of computers and the like. 'And you've been seeing signs of poaching, small but regular. That set me thinking. I had a printout made of the petty crimes for the past few years. Discounting the ones we've solved and the obviously irrelevant, an interesting pattern showed up, starting at least a year ago, probably longer.' He flipped over some folds of his paper, scowled at it and scratched his neck. 'There's been some thefts of lingerie from washing lines, but we can guess who that is.'

'Oh?' Deborah said quickly. 'Who?'

'That is neither here nor there,' Ian said. 'The point is that men's clothes are now being taken from the lines if the housewife's careless enough to leave them out overnight, and that is unusual. Also sometimes towels and even the lines themselves. Milk

17

and rolls from doorsteps and the occasional news-paper. And thefts from cars are up again, but this time joyriders aren't to blame, the cars themselves are still there in the morning. Two car rugs. Shotgun cartridges, always either twelve-bore or four-ten – which is worrying, but they may not be connected. The list goes on and on and sometimes it's difficult to see what's relevant and what's not. And, of course, God alone knows what else has gone for a walk and not been reported. If something vanishes from his garden shed the average man doesn't come running to the police, he wonders where he left it and eventually buys another one. The point is that what the pattern adds up to in my mind is somebody living rough.'

'Could be,' Deborah said. 'But in the case of the man we saw, I rather doubt it.'

'Why?'

'I told you,' she said, 'that I smelled rabbit on him and nothing else. I'd been sniffing the air, remember, waiting for the scent of a fox, so I was sort of attuned.'

Ian looked puzzled. 'And so?'

'And so this. When a man's living rough, he doesn't have many chances to take a bath or to get his laundry washed. I'd expect more than a trace of BO.'

'And there wasn't?'

Deborah looked at me. 'I wouldn't know,' I said. 'He was gone before Deborah's scream had died away.'

The reason for my glance at my uncle was that I was wondering how to explain tactfully that his presence had made it difficult to be quite sure. Uncle Ronnie takes a bath at least once a week – whether he needs it or not, he says – but the nature of his job is such that his clothes usually carry the odour of something dead, often of fish. Mum has his suits cleaned whenever she can get her hands on them but it only takes an hour in his Land-Rover, which is impregnated with the aftermath of the kill, for them to pick up the scent again. And I never scream. I may have uttered an exclamation of surprise, but I definitely did not scream.

'Well,' Ian said, 'it's a point. But there are several vacant cottages within a walkable distance; and houses are sometimes unoccupied while the owners are away. He may have broken in and treated himself to a wash and a change of clothing. I'll have a few enquiries made.'

'I'd better take a look at the bothy,' I said. Our main fishing is up in the north-west and we only have a bit of a river within reach of Newton Lauder, a tributary of the Tweed; but there's a small hut for the use of fishermen, with benches and a bottled gas stove. It's in a secluded place and a man could live there in comfort while the gas lasted. Nobody would have been near it for months. Salmon were back in season but you hardly ever see a fish hereabouts until much later in the year and the local brown trout season was still weeks away.

'And I'll ask the farmers to look around their outbuildings for signs of occupation,' Sir Peter said. 'It starts with sleeping rough but it often ends with serious burglary or fire-raising.'

'Sometimes even violence, if he's disturbed,' Ian

said. He nodded sombrely. 'Warn them to have a care. I think that's about as far as we can take it for the moment.'

'Oh? You don't want to know his identity?' Deborah asked.

We gaped at her. 'You know it?' Ian asked.

'No.' Ian opened his mouth again to make some scathing comment but she went on quickly. 'There's a chance you might get it. He grabbed at the gun as he went by and got a grip on it at the muzzles, but I wasn't going to let him get away with my uncle's gun so I hung on. He's damn lucky that my finger wasn't on the trigger or he'd have blown his head off. Then he lost his grip and went on. If he is, as you think he is, living rough, there's a good chance his fingerprints are on file.'

Ian brightened slightly. 'It's possible. And I suppose some prints may have survived, if the gun hasn't been cleaned since.'

'That's my magnum she's talking about,' I said. 'It hadn't been fired. What for would I clean it? It's been in the gunsafe all the while I was up north.'

'It's a slim chance,' Ian said. 'If the barrels were dragged out of his fingers, the prints would be smeared. But it's certainly worth a try. Leave the gun with me, as soon as you can. And we'll keep in touch.'

When we were back in the Land-Rover, Sir Peter said, 'I think we'll just go and take that look at the bothy.'

I could have been better employed getting on with my job or Young Hamish's but, when the boss calls, you go. Sir Peter drove up towards the moor and then took to a rough track that wound its way up

20

and over a shoulder and then downhill to the river. It's smaller than many a trout stream in places, but salmon come up in summer, ready to mate and lay their eggs in the shingle that autumn, so it's a river. It's a funny old language. We talk about a salmon river and a trout stream and they may be the same bit of water.

I was surprised at the amount of light on the water. I mostly see it in the fishing season when the leaves are on the trees so that my recollection is of a dimness and shelter. As soon as we came in sight, I could see that the bothy door had been forced. The gas stove was still in place but there was no sign of the cylinders and regulators which had been there when we locked the door back in the autumn. Luckily the cylinders could not have held much gas. I'm not a believer of leaving full cylinders around. There was no sign that the place had been slept in.

'You'd better tell young Ian,' Sir Peter said.

'Aye. And I'll get new gas cylinders?'

'I suppose so. Can't have you going without your supper,' he said sadly. 'But get the door mended first.'

TWO

Next morning, I dropped my gun-barrels off with Ian and picked up Deborah from their flat. She was wearing heavy boots, ripped jeans and a cast-off sweater of Ian's. A muirburn is definitely not an occasion for dressing up.

A small flock of about twenty sheep fled across the heather as we arrived, then clumped together and looked back at us resentfully, as if wondering what all the fuss had been about. Grouse cost more than twice as much to shoot as pheasants, although the keepering cost is not much greater and they breed in the wild and feed themselves on the heather. In my book, the main cost is that the number of sheep on a moor has to be kept very low. A few sheep help to keep open some tracks where the birds can sun themselves, but an economic flock soon ruins the heather. I sometimes wonder how long our heather moorlands would last if grouse shooting ever stopped, and how many other species would die out with the grouse. Folk just don't realize the contribution that shooting pressures make to the environment.

Sir Peter and Young Hamish were looking over the scene with satisfaction. The brush cutter had already isolated the strips of older heather to be burned. There was a breeze. The heather was neither too damp nor too dry. Four other helpers had turned out so it was decided that we could safely keep two strips burning at a time.

A muirburn is hot and uncomfortable work, but we were well equipped with visors and our 'beaters' were ten-foot poles with rubber squares on the end. The work was made easier by the firebreaks cut by the brush cutter but, while the old and degenerate heather was mostly within the strips to be burned, some of it was to be left to provide winter feeding for the grouse if deep snow should come, and a spark blowing that way could have us cursing and sweating for a quarter of an hour until all was under control again.

Sir Peter's High Moor is small as moors go. By dusk, we had broken the back of it. One more morning should see it finished for another season. Deborah and I walked back over what we had done to be sure that the peat was not still smouldering. The others were gathered at the last strip, beating at the dying flames.

From a quarter-mile away, the first sound was inaudible. The first that we heard, very faintly, was some shouting followed by the sound of a shot. Then there was more shouting. The ordered movements of the other party had disintegrated, and not to cope with a sudden escape of the flames. We hurried back in that direction. One man was beating at the still smouldering heather but the others had gathered together and when we had detoured around the end of the fire and joined them we found that they were grouped around Young Hamish, who was down in

23

the short heather and bellowing like a stag in rut.

Sir Peter was looking around in a bemused way. 'Hamish has been shot,' he said.

'But nobody had a gun,' I pointed out. 'Unless somebody fetched one from the cars?'

He shook his head emphatically. 'Nothing like that.'

Sir Peter's head forester was down on his knees beside Hamish. 'There's no doubt about it being shot,' he said. 'These are pellet holes. But it came from the fire. I saw the sparks fly. We heard a pop and Hamish fell down. The bang came later. I'm damned if I can make any sense of it.'

'A discarded cartridge?' Sir Peter suggested.

'A cartridge only burns, outside of a gun,' I said.

'We'll worry later about who or what caused it,' said Sir Peter. 'The first thing is to get Hamish to hospital.'

Deborah had ripped a strip of cloth from somewhere about her person and was tying up what looked like a nasty wound on Hamish's knee. The cars had been left where we had parked my Land-Rover on the night of our strange encounter, no great distance away. The forester linked hands with me and with Hamish sitting on them we carried him there. He had stopped his roaring now that he was sure that his leg was still attached, but his moans whenever we stumbled were pitiful.

'Put him in my Land-Rover,' Sir Peter said. 'I'll take him to hospital and come back. You'd better stay here and see to the fire. Unless ... Have you had enough, Deborah? I could drop you at home. You must be exhausted.'

Deborah was looking over her shoulder. 'I think

all hands are going to be needed here,' she said, and I saw that a new breeze was picking up the fire in one or two places.

'By George, yes,' Sir Peter said. 'I'll be back as soon as I can.'

The Land-Rover eased its way gently down the track and we hurried back to find that the fire was in danger of getting out of control. With six of us beating, it still took half an hour of choking work to settle it down. We were glad of a breather by the time it was reduced to a smoking stubble. Suddenly, it had become dark while we were too busy to notice. There was no glow over the castle, I was relieved to see, but the night was clear and on such nights the glow was rarely seen.

The flasks of tea were empty but I had some beer in my Land-Rover. I walked to fetch half a dozen cans and at the same time I collected my new lamp. On the way back, I took a look along the dry-stone wall where Deborah and I had sat and about thirty yards downwind I found what, after some thought, I realized that I might have expected all along – the half-eaten corpse of a rabbit in a snare which had been set in a gap in the wall. That explained why the man, whoever he was, had come towards my squeaking.

My uncle would die rather than admit it, but I know that we were each secretly relieved by this sign that the visitation had not been supernatural.

Sir Peter returned while we were washing the smoke out of our throats. (The foresters had even lit cigarettes!) With him he brought Ian, Deborah's husband. Hamish, he said, was sedated and the damage to his leg was being attended to. Opinion was that the damage would heal in time.

The head forester pointed out the place where he thought the shot had come from. The ashes there were cooling enough to allow a search. I shone the lamp. We all had a good look around. It was Deborah who stopped suddenly and pointed. I brought the lamp over.

Lying among the ashes, sooty and charred, was the remains of a small shotgun; a pump-action gun of about four-ten or maybe twenty-eight-bore was my guess. It seemed to have been fitted with some kind of a silencer or sound moderator and the tubular magazine was ripped open.

'That certainly accounts for it,' Deborah said. We waited respectfully. She is the firearms expert. 'The pop that was heard first of all was the round in the chamber going off. That'll be what peppered Hamish. Then the rounds in the magazine exploded in a chain reaction.'

'It doesn't explain why somebody abandoned a shotgun in the heather,' Ian said. 'We've had no reports of somebody laying down a gun and not being able to find it again.'

'I'll bet that it was left by our apparition,' Deborah said. 'If he suspected that we were lurking he might have stashed the gun in the heather so as not to risk being charged with a firearms offence.'

'Why didn't he come back for it?' I asked.

'Maybe he did, but couldn't find where he'd hidden it – in the dark, remember. I don't know that I could hide a gun in the heather by night and find it again later.'

'Could be.' Ian took the lamp from me and moved off, breaking the connection to the battery in my pocket. We were plunged into darkness. When light was restored he shone the lamp around. 'Any other evidence has gone up with the smoke,' he said. 'I don't suppose it matters. We've no reason to believe that a crime was committed here. I'll take charge of the gun for the moment and see if the owner can be traced. He'll have some explaining to do. My revered father-in-law may have some useful comments to make.'

'And—' Deborah began.

'And my even more revered and slightly beloved wife,' Ian added quickly. I heard one of the foresters chuckle in the darkness.

Keith's shop has a dignified, old-fashioned look about the front. I mind that it was a jeweller's before Keith took it over and whatever changes he may have made he managed to keep it the very picture of affluent respectability. Now, behind that front, it's jam-packed with shooting and fishing tackle and clothing, arranged as neatly as you can manage when there isn't really room to be as methodical as you'd like. I was in need of some cartridges and a sink-tip fly-line; and by chance I reached the shop when Ian had just brought the ruined shotgun in.

'By chance' is good! Sheer nosiness. I could see Uncle Ron hanging around in the Square, waiting for Ian to arrive, while I was discussing one or two repair jobs with Dad.

Keith's partner, Wallace, was away on a winter

break with his wife. Keith, who more often works at home on gun repairs and dealing in vintage weapons, was minding the shop while Deborah was hanging around, not wanting to miss the excitement. Keith's a good-looking devil still, although he now has the sort of 'elder statesman' looks suggesting a man of maturity fit to be trusted. In his younger days, parents of daughters took one look and decided not to trust him an inch.

On the shop counter, which stood in a clear space dwarfed by the racks and shelves towering around, Ian was unwrapping the gun from a polythene sheet when I came in. Deborah slipped past me to hang the 'Closed' sign on the door.

'What do you make of this?' Ian asked Keith.

Keith lifted the gun. The woodwork was badly charred and the metal twisted. 'Found in the burned heather?' he said. 'Deborah told me about it. She's been up to the hospital and Hamish is going into surgery about now for the removal of the pellets. And I'll tell you something else for nothing. This'll never fire again. Let's have a look. It is, or was, a pump-action four-ten by... Armas Alicante, wouldn't you say?'

'That's what I thought,' said Deborah.

'Four-ten's about the smallest gauge, isn't it?' Ian asked.

'The smallest in anything like common use. Did you get a number off it?'

Ian shook his head. 'We didn't know where to look and we didn't want to clean the whole gun in case there was something else to be learned from it.'

Keith fetched a small wad of wire wool from the back shop and rubbed gently at an area above the trigger. 'I don't remember ever selling one of these,' he said. 'They never caught on. Ah, here we are.' He read out a number comprising a letter and five digits.

Ian picked up the shop phone, raised his eyebrows, got a nod in reply, dialled his office and relayed the number to his sergeant. 'Ferless will call me here if it figures on anybody's shotgun certificate.'

'It won't,' Keith said. Ian looked at him enquiringly but Keith was looking into the tubular magazine which was split open from end to end. 'The magazine has never been adapted to suit the new legislation, which only allows for a maximum of two in the magazine plus one up the spout. This seems to have had four in the magazine, plus one. If it's legally held it'll be as a firearm, not a shotgun. Better try the list of stolen guns.'

Ian dialled again and gave Sergeant Ferless fresh instructions. A fat man with a gunbag over his shoulder was rapping on the door and peering through the glass. Deborah shook her head at him.

'One last thing,' Keith said quickly. 'The sound moderator isn't a stock item. It's neatly made but it's a one-off. Not a difficult job, given a piece of tubing, a lot of cup-washers and the right tools. The threads might tell you what sort of mechanic did the work. And now . . .'

'I'll take my unprofitable self away and leave you to get on with the day's business,' Ian agreed. I'll be in touch.'

The man on the doorstep looked with curiosity at the bundle Ian was carrying. He brought in a shotgun for cleaning and overhaul. Deborah served me but was called away by the phone. She darted to

29

the door and I heard her calling. Ian returned, again crossing with Keith's client in the doorway.

'Your sergeant's back on the phone,' Deborah said. She locked the door again and finished making up my order while Ian took the call.

'Well, I'll be damned,' Ian said at last, hanging up. He smiled suddenly at his wife. 'Your thought paid off,' he told her. 'We don't have a fingerprint section here – the work usually has to be dealt with from Edinburgh. But one of my constables did the course and I let him try himself out on this for the sake of the experience, because I didn't think there was a hope in hell of getting a clear print or of the print being on record if we did.

'But there were three good, clear prints on the greased barrels of your gun, Ronnie. My lad couldn't match them in what I call the mainstream files so, being keen almost to excess, he searched the prints that I insist on being retained as backup, just in case. After all, a crook may be abroad or in jug or dead but his latent prints can still turn up somewhere, even years later.'

'That was no dead man,' Deborah said.

'So it seems.'

'And my gun was cleaned only a day or two before,' I added hotly, in case he was insinuating that the fingerprints had been in place for months. 'Who was it?'

'Somebody who might well have been dead, although the official view was that he had slipped abroad.' Ian scratched his neck, a sign that he was deep in thought.

'Anybody we'd know?' Keith asked.

'It's possible.' Ian paused for further thought. 'This

30

is Friday,' he said at last. 'I need the weekend to do some homework. And to consider whether it's something I should hand over to my bosses in Edinburgh. But if I decide to look into it, I'll be grateful for some local knowledge, quite likely going back to long before I came to Newton Lauder. Would the three of you be free on Monday morning?'

'I can't promise,' Keith said.

'Sunday evening, then? Come to us for drinks . . . after dinner.' He was watching his wife out of the corner of his eye.

Deborah heaved a sigh. 'I can take a hint,' she said. 'Come about seven and I'll throw some food on the table. That is, if Mum can come too?' she added to Ian.

Ian nodded. 'She knows as many guilty secrets as the rest of you put together,' he said, 'but she can keep a confidence when she has to.'

Although Deborah made a show of resenting the chore of making a Sunday dinner for three guests, she enjoys entertaining in her new home and she's beginning to cook almost as well as her mum.

Well, thank you!

What's more, she makes her own wines, which I'm told are almost as good as the real thing. I wouldn't know about that. I'm a beer and whisky man myself.

We had a grand meal, if a bit on the fancy side, but it was pheasant – from the freezer, I'll be bound, because the season was over – and Deborah gave me a leg with my helping. The one trick she's never mastered, although Molly and I between us must have told her a thousand times how to do it, is to break the bird's leg just below what seems like the knee (but is really the ankle) and give a good jerk so that the foot comes away with all those sinews that become like thin bones when the bird's cooked. Whenever I have a bad dream it's that I'm at a posh dinner and seated alongside the queen and I have a badly prepared leg to deal with. There's no way you can manage it without using your fingers. Keith had brought along a bottle of the special whisky he gets from a Customs mannie at one of the distilleries. Ian refused to speak about lost shotguns and vanished men living rough until we moved through for coffee and mints, by which time we were all in a good mood.

My uncle's mood was so good that I could only be thankful that Dad had given him a lift. I don't think that he need worry about being asked to dine with Her Majesty. And it isn't that I don't know how to prepare a pheasant properly, it's that I can't bring myself to do it. I can't help thinking that if they'd been bigger and cleverer than we are, one of them might have been jerking my leg off.

They had papered one wall of the living-room and introduced some bonny splashes of colour, so that the fresh-from-the-builders look had been replaced by something more homelike.

A silence seemed to fall of its own accord and we all looked at Ian.

'I've been reading up the records of a certain

case,' he said, 'but the men who made them up already knew all the background. Nobody ever writes down what everybody knows. I'm hoping that, between you, you can help me to get the picture. The case has been officially closed and all that I have to go on at the moment is the recovery of a stolen shotgun and indications of a man living rough, so I don't feel obliged to invoke my chiefs in Edinburgh and there's no reason why I shouldn't discuss it with you . . . in confidence.'

'Then for God's sake do it and stop beating about the bush,' Deborah said.

'When you're not here, she beats me cruelly,' Ian said in an aside. Keith and Molly both smiled, but I'd have been half prepared to believe him. 'The shotgun found on the moor had originally belonged to one Steven Forester, a company director resident in Edinburgh but since moved to London. That's not particularly relevant. What is relevant is that it was in the boot of his Lancia when the car was stolen, not far from here. The car was never recovered.'

'Oho!' Deborah said, and I realized that Ian had told her nothing of what we were about to hear.

'How long ago was that?' Keith asked.

'Between three and four years ago.'

A stolen car might suggest a connection with Nathaniel Connerty.'

'Quite possibly,' Ian said. 'Remember, much of the Nat Connerty story happened before I came here, and when I arrived I was only a token CID presence at first, a mere sergeant, with anything of the least interest still being handled from Edinburgh. By the time the case broke I had been made up to

33

inspector, but the case belonged to the Fraud Squad.

'Nat Connerty was a local boy. He started life here and finished it less than twenty miles away. Between you, you must know more of the background than ever appeared in the files. So put the flesh on the bones of his story for me, will you?'

'How far back do you want us to go?' I asked.

'As far as you can.'

'I can go as far back as you want. I remember him as a boy,' I said. 'He was a year ahead of me so I never saw a lot of him at the school, but we both went beating on Saturdays in season. Much later, he was turning up as a guest or a member on some of the same shoots, but I was still a beater.'

'Were you surprised that he got on in the world?' Ian asked.

I thought about it and decided that I wasn't. 'Not really. He aye had the knack of looking you straight in the eye and telling a barefaced, black, bloody lie and usually getting away with it. When he was caught out, he would shrug and smile and explain one lie away with three more, and somehow you'd let it go. One of his teachers said that he was born to be a politician or a second-hand car salesman.'

'And, as it happened, he was both,' said Keith.

'His first job was with one of the big garages in Edinburgh,' Molly said. 'He was walking out with a friend of mine at the time. From what she said, he always had more money than you'd have expected, so he must have been up to something even then.'

'He was,' Keith said. 'I don't know what, but it was in the nature of the man always to be "up to" something. He must have scraped some capital together soon after that, because he bought a scrap-

34

yard outside Edinburgh that also traded in old bangers. You know the kind of deal. Buying in scrapped vehicles and getting some of them back on the road by taking good parts off the others. I went there once to follow up one of his advertisements, but when I saw what was going on I turned round and drove away again – but not before Nat had tried to convince me that a worn-out wreck that I recognized as having been one of Ledbetter's taxis had had one careful lady owner. He must have worn his arm out winding back milometers.

'Soon, he bought another garage, a more reputable one. And from them on, there was no stopping him. It was the old game of borrowing against one business to buy the next. It was as if he wanted to get a stranglehold on the private car market for southern Scotland. But he was into hire cars and rentals and leasing as well. It was becoming an empire.

'I mentioned him to Wallace once while we were having one of our usual arguments about expanding our own business. Wal just laughed and said that Nat was due to come badly unstuck one of those days. You know how Wal understands money the way a gardener understands plants. He'd been to one of Nat's showrooms when his old Fiat was on its last legs, because Nat was giving good discounts on new cars and advertising better credit and trade-in terms than anybody else.

'When Wal saw the kind of deal they offered him he jumped at it but, Wal being Wal, he was careful to pay for the car on the spot, by cheque, and he not only kept his receipt but he also got his bank to return the cancelled cheque to him. He said that if a business that was operating on borrowed capital could give those terms and survive he was a monkey's uncle, and he was ready to bet that they were fiddling the hire-purchase agreements. Sure enough, when the muck finally hit the fan a finance company tried to repossess his car; but he had cast-iron proof that he'd paid cash and the signature on the hire-purchase form was only a crude imitation of his writing.

'Meantime, the Connerty empire seemed to be going on from strength to strength and Nat himself spared no pains to drag himself, and his wife when he got one, into both the gentry and the jet set. Nat even raced sports cars for a while. People wondered where all the money was coming from, but in hindsight the cars probably came free. When Nat got married, he seemed to settle down. He was a regional councillor for several years. He bought Gillespie House and the estate that went with it and set himself up as a local laird. He worked up a small shoot on his land, doing most of the work himself but aided part-time by a retired keeper. I was invited to shoot there two or three times.'

'You'll know Nat's half-brother then,' I said. 'Bruce.'

'No,' Keith said. 'He never got involved in the shoot at all.'

'I heard that he moved in with the Lacy sisters at Skerriden,' I said.

Nobody seemed interested in Bruce Connerty's sex life.

'Nat, I remember, bought himself a pair of German shorthaired pointers and had them professionally trained,' Keith said. 'He called them

36

Castor and Pollux after the Heavenly Twins – his birth sign. They were blood brothers, but Castor was by far the better dog and Nat's favourite so, Sod's Law being what it is, it was Castor that ripped himself on some barbed wire, took blood poisoning and died. And Nat got fed up keeping a dog that could barely recognize its own name and with having to call out "Pollux" in the street, which was earning him some funny looks, so he gave the surviving dog away.

'Whenever the subject of Nat Connerty came up, I used to ask after the health of Wal's nephew Simian, but Wal only smiled in a superior way. He said that interest rates were shooting up and that it was only a matter of time.'

'There were some whispers,' I put in.

Keith nodded. 'There were indeed,' he said. 'About ringers and, latterly, about stolen cars. One car that had passed through Nat's hands was in a smash and broke in half – the front half of a stolen car had been welded to the back half of a vehicle that had been front-ended and written off. A fore-man was jugged and it seemed to blow over.'

'That was Harry Fury,' Molly said. 'He lived here although he worked near Edinburgh. And I'll tell you something else. Even while he was in prison, his family never went short of anything.'

'I suppose he was paid to take the rap for every-body else,' Deborah said.

'That's for sure,' said Keith. 'Is he still inside?'

He wasn't in for very long at all,' said Molly. 'I was seeing him around again before Nat Connerty's death. But he was unemployed by then. So that doesn't look as though he was part of a larger fiddle.'

37

'From what I heard,' Keith said, 'he was calling down extravagant curses on Nat's head. I suspect that Nat kept him sweet until he'd served his time and then, when it was too late for anything Harry Fury said to do Nat any real damage, he got rid of him.'

'You'd believe anything bad about Nat Connerty,' Deborah said.

'Maybe. For several years more, things seemed to roll along. Thefts of cars were on the increase and none of them was ever recovered. It was said later that most of them were on the way to foreign parts before they were missed, in the care of Nat's personal chauffeur and dogsbody. And then, suddenly, nearly two years ago, Nat and another man were dead in separate accidents, it was safe to leave your car in a dark street again and everybody said that he'd been propping up his businesses by heading a stolen car racket. Wallace,' Keith added, 'was insufferable for a fortnight.

'And that was almost the end of the story, except that Nat's death was never properly explained. And there was some mystery as to where all the money went.'

'The widow probably has it tucked away somewhere,' Molly said, looking at Keith out of the corner of her eye.

'I doubt that,' Keith said. 'The house and estate had been gifted to her much earlier, but even so I hear that she's been living hand to mouth there ever since, and very quietly.'

That was almost true if you accept that the quiet

life includes a succession of local scandals about male weekend guests who sometimes stayed on for weeks. An old schoolfriend of mine lives near by and was in the habit of ringing up to tell me the latest.

At this point in the manuscript a full half-page had been heavily deleted, probably just after my uncle realized that I was going to vet his original work. But Uncle Ronnie need not have bothered. I had known for years that Jacinthe, the widow of Nat Connerty, had been one of the loves of Dad's disreputable youth. So what? I never took up a moral stance about my dad's past. It was simply one of the facts. Mum's attitude is much the same. He has been a good husband and father and that's enough.

Ian had been listening in silence. 'Well, thank you,' he said suddenly. 'You've been very helpful. I'll get back to you if there are any more gaps to be filled.' He looked at his watch, hinting that it was time that guests were on their way.

Molly and Deborah made indignant noises and Keith said, 'Oh no you don't! Did you think that you could pick our brains and hint that Nat Connerty was still alive and living rough around here and then tell us to run along?'

Ian shrugged and grinned. 'It was worth a try,' he said. 'My job is to gather information, not to hand it out. But, in confidence . . . it's no wonder that I couldn't find a consolidated source for the background. When the case was shelved, the records would have been split between a whole lot of files

– fraud, car theft, unnatural death and God alone knows what else. When did I ever say that the fingerprints on Ronnie's gun were Nat Connerty's?'

'You seemed to be hinting in that direction,' Keith said. 'And knowing what a crafty devil Nat was, I wouldn't be at all surprised if he skipped abroad, leaving some other poor sod to substitute for his corpse. As I remember it, his car slid on wet leaves, hit a tree and burned. The fiscal called a Fatal Accident Inquiry, but some other idiot topped himself in the same neighbourhood and that rather squeezed Nat off what was left of the front page of the local rag after they'd printed all the really important news about Local Boy Makes Good and New Look For Town Hall. From the sloppy and garbled report that found its way into print it was difficult to be sure how the charred remains had been identified. There was no mention of dental evidence.'

'Nat was always terrified of dentists,' I said.

I could see that Ian was laughing at us up his sleeve. 'Whose body did you think it might have been?' he asked.

'There was the half-brother,' Molly said tentatively.

'Bruce,' I reminded her. 'A bit slow, not to say thick. And a rough customer.' I paused, but nobody made any funny remarks. 'Nat used him as a collector of bad debts and a repo man when customers couldn't keep up with the hire purchase. But he was shorter than Nat.'

'My money would have been on Nat's Financial Director, Winchester or some such, for the substitute,' Keith said. 'If substitute there was.'

'Wincherly,' Ian said. 'Julian Wincherly.'

Keith snapped his fingers. 'That's the man,' he

said. 'I met him once when I was invited to some motor-trade dinner. The same build as Nat, medium height and rather thickset. And because he'd let Nat bury himself so deep in the financial muck, I could well imagine Nat leaving him behind to distract attention from himself.'

'You're off the beam there,' Ian said. 'There's a statement on file from Mr Wincherly to the effect that he was just going to turn into the drive when he saw Mr Connerty drive off, seconds before the smash. He was very nearly prosecuted for his part in the swindles, but he had a whole lot of copies of memos he'd sent to Connerty, warning him not to do this or that, and the fiscal said that the case wasn't worth pursuing. He gave evidence at the inquiry.'

'Oh,' said Keith. He never spends more than a few minutes on a daily paper and even then most of his attention is given to the advertisements.

'But he might not have told the truth,' Deborah pointed out. 'He might have agreed with Nat to fake Nat's death and join him abroad and split the money, whatever was left of it.'

'Then whose body was it?' Ian asked, still with a glint of amusement in his eye.

'The chauffeur and dogsbody,' Keith said. 'Dougie something. Slattery, that was it. Dougie Slattery.'

'Very good,' Ian said. 'When my colleagues searched the house they gathered up several false passports in the rooms Slattery occupied over the garage. It turned out that he'd been making two trips a week to the continent, driving stolen cars on false plates. As far as is known, he hasn't been seen since.'

'There you are, then,' said Keith.

41

I had been sitting mostly quiet and listening to them, but it seemed to be my turn to speak up. 'No, you aren't,' I said.

'Why not?' Keith asked indignantly.

'Ian's leading you on. I grew up alongside Dougie,' I told him. 'You'll remember, Molly. He lived in one of those railwaymen's cottages – leastways, they were when there was still a railway – about half a mile from us.'

My sister put her nose in the air. 'I remember the cottages. I never had anything to do with the people. You were the one who mixed with tinkies and roughs.'

'Dougie was all right,' I said, not really meaning it. Dougie had always been wild. What I meant was that his good points were more important than his bad. 'His dad was Irish, a man who understood nature better than anyone I ever met, and Dougie took after him. Everything I know about deer and birds and fish – well, almost everything – I learned from those two. Dougie was almost as good as his dad. He could guddle a trout, snare a fox or go through a wood without even the birds knowing he'd been there, let alone the keeper. And I thought my night vision was good, but Dougie's was better. Nat went along with him sometimes, but he never had the magic touch that Dougie had.

'Later on, when cars caught his interest, he was just as good with machinery. Nat should have let Dougie drive the sports cars, not tried to do it himself. They might have had more wins and fewer dunts and breakages.'

'So Dougie was a good driver,' Keith said impatiently. 'He was the one who whipped stolen cars abroad, the ones that weren't kept here and ringed. What of it?'

'So this,' I said. 'Unless Ian's tricking us, the man we met on the moor was connected with Nat Connerty. If there was ever a man who could hole up and live off the land without anybody knowing he was there, it was Dougie.'

'Unless he was the corpse in the car,' Keith said. 'If Nat hung around with you and Dougie in his boyhood, he would have learned enough to poach a few rabbits and game-birds.'

'And fish,' I said.

'And fish. He could lift all the vegetables he'd need out of fields and gardens. And when he wanted a corpse to take the heat off himself, he was quite ruthless enough to use an old friend for the purpose.'

'I go along with Uncle Ron,' Deborah said suddenly. 'For one thing, Mr Connerty was a successful man even if he didn't exactly toe the legal line. Anything weird that's connected with stolen cars and his name's bound to come up, but I can't see him living rough and using a gun that came out of one of those stolen cars. But one of his minions, yes. Then again, the reporting was abysmal, as Dad said. The local rag had an editor at that time who went in for nepotism in a big way. The paper was staffed entirely by his aunts and cousins, none of whom could string a coherent sentence together. But soon after the smash, at some party or other, I met the couple who witnessed it. They live right at the bend of the road where it happened and they'd just come out of the house to walk the dogs. They said that the car was coming away from the direction of Gillespie House, going south at a rate of knots, and hit a patch of wet leaves. The car slid, the driver didn't even try to correct and the car went into the trees. The fuel caught instantly.'

'That's true,' Ian said. 'It doesn't usually happen, despite what you see in the movies, but this time a combination of wiring damage with a stump ripping the pipe off the tank seems to have turned the car into a fire-bomb.'

'My point,' Deboroh said, 'is that you couldn't fake that sort of accident without leaving signs of sabotage and, from what Dad said, Dougie Slattery was too good a driver to have been caught that way.'

What I didn't say, for fear of leading the discussion onto dangerous ground, was that Mrs Connerty's behaviour supported my uncle's theory rather than Dad's. If Dougie had died in the burning car, both Mr Connerty and the missing assets would still have been around and the supposed widow would hardly have been eking out an impoverished existence by sleeping with friends and strangers. Unless, of course, the ruthless Mr Connerty had been escaping from an unsatisfactory marriage as well as from the law and his creditors, but from what I remembered of her from her days in Newton Lauder she was not the type of woman to let a good husband get away from her.

Keith thought it over for a few seconds before he spoke. 'We don't have to argue about it,' he said to Ian. 'Whose were the fingerprints on Ronnie's gun? Nat's or Dougie's?'

Ian, who was going round again with the bottles,

straightened up, grinning all over his face. 'I'd be delighted to be able to confound you by saying that they belonged to neither man. But, in fact, they were Dougie Slattery's.'

While Molly's eyes were on the glass that she was holding out to Ian I gave Keith a two-fingered salute, but Molly always did have eyes in the back of her head. 'Be nice, Ronnie,' she said, 'or go home. So it really was Nat in the car? Or is there still some doubt about that?'

'I'm sorry to spoil a good mystery, but it was Nathaniel Connerty in the car,' said Ian. 'His doctor dug out an X-ray dating from when he broke his hip in a racing crash. The corpse showed signs of an identical fracture.'

'And the money burned up with him?' Molly persisted. 'Or was there any money? Had it all been swallowed up by the business losses?'

'There should have been money,' Ian said, 'and a lot of it. I can give you back a part of your mystery. Several of the ringers – the stolen cars – had come to light when it was found that the chassis numbers had been tampered with, and they had all gone through one or another of Nat's outlets. The investigation was closing in and he must have known it, because he stopped paying his suppliers and made large withdrawals in cash. That would have been on top of whatever cash Dougie Slattery had regularly been bringing back from the Continent.

'Things suddenly came to a head – on a Saturday, as I remember. Plans had been laid for Nat's arrest and for simultaneous swoops on his various businesses in order to catch as many of his minions as possible in the act of doctoring stolen vehicles.

Ringing tends to be an after-hours activity, to exclude any employees who aren't known to be bent.

'Extra officers had been brought in at the last minute for the purpose. By ill luck one of those men had been on Nat's payroll, doing him little favours like feeding false information into the Vehicle Licensing Centre computer. But, by a counterbalancing stroke of good luck, somebody heard him phoning Nat to warn him that his arrest was imminent.

'By yet more ill luck for me, I was left behind in charge of the culprit with orders to keep him absolutely incommunicado. So I missed all the excitement, and what little I know from here on is hearsay or from reading the reports.

'The cars were sent out immediately and the arresting party was at Gillespie House within twenty minutes; but they missed Nat Connerty by ten. Dougie Slattery had faded quietly away during the same interval in Mrs Connerty's BMW. That car turned up in Newcastle, but it had earlier been stolen and put through the ringing process, so eventually it went back to its original owners. Mrs Connerty and the cook-housekeeper, a Mrs Jablinska, were alone in the house and they swore that Nat had bolted as soon as he got the phone call.

'The remains of Nat's car were given a thorough going-over, as you can imagine. There was no sign of tampering, nor of any money. The fuel pipe had fractured at the first impact. A spark from the wiring ignited the fuel. The tank never went up – they usually don't, except on the telly, but on this occasion more and more fuel escaped to feed the flames. The car burned thoroughly, but the kind of money that we were looking for would make a solid slab of paper; and paper doesn't burn completely if the air can't get around it. There would surely have been some traces left if it had been in the car.'

'And Dougie doesn't have it,' Keith said, 'or he'd have used one of his false passports and headed for the sunshine.'

Ian shrugged and pulled a face. 'Until now, it was assumed that Dougie carried the money abroad for Nat Connerty, who never turned up to collect it. My own bet would have been that Slattery was living a life of brandy and cigars and silken dalliance with ladies of the night; but now it begins to look as though Connerty was on the way to pick up his money when he wrote himself off. In which case either the pal who was holding it for him has been enjoying the fruits of Nat's frauds or else the money's buried in the woods and quietly rotting away.'

We were silent for a minute – a one-minute silence out of respect for something precious rotting in a lonely grave, which was more than we had given for the late Nat. When the conversation resumed it seemed that we had moved on.

'Whose was the other body?' Keith asked. 'No connection with the late Nat Connerty? That would be too much of a coincidence to swallow.'

'A very definite connection,' Ian said. 'Mr Daniel Graham. He and his wife were acquaintances of the Connertys. They had invested a lot of money in Nat's various enterprises.

'He was found next morning at the bottom of a quarry rock-face but it seemed that he might very well have fallen, jumped or been pushed at about the time of Nat's death, give or take an hour or two. The sheriff brought it in as suicide.'

'You don't sound very convinced,' Deborah said.

'If I don't,' said Ian, 'perhaps it's because I'm not.'
He went round with the bottle again and, truth to
tell, I don't remember much of what was said after
that.

THREE

It was a busy period for me. I had to hurry north once. The season for red deer was over, but there was another party of fishers and Wullie was bad with the flu. Although Hamish was back on his feet he was unfit to do more than hobble around on a crutch and most of my time went on doing his job for him, tending snares and lamping for a vixen that seemed to have come onto the land intent on setting up a den. Between times I was humping feed to the pheasant feeders and grit to the moor and getting the release pens into shape for the arrival of poults later in the year. We planned to buy pheasant poults at six weeks old that year instead of rearing our own.

What with acting as stand-in keeper and keeping the roe deer down to acceptable numbers, I had little time even to think about Dougie and Nat, but I kept my eyes and ears open. The signs were there – rabbit snares hidden deep in the bushes, a cock pheasant choking on a raisin with a horsehair threaded through it, scattered pigeon feathers. I noticed that a full hundredweight of potatoes had vanished from the clamp behind my house and another gardener complained that his Brussels sprouts had been stripped in the night.

The area around Newton Lauder is dotted with cottages once occupied by farmworkers, foresters and quarrymen and some of these were vacant or had been converted into holiday cottages and were standing empty. Ian must have been following the same train of thought because I kept seeing his Bobbies visiting the empty ones or poking into the remoter outbuildings on the farms. But there were no signs of illicit occupation. If somebody was living rough, I decided, he was living very rough indeed.

One day, on the by-road leading up to a farmhouse, I came up behind a slow figure and recognized a retired farmer who now managed for himself in a refurbished cottar-house while his son ran the farm and raised a brood of kids there. The old man had a collie at heel, as full of years as himself. It was a raw day and they still had a stiff climb before them so I stopped and offered a lift. The old man nodded. He looked doubtfully at my Land-Rover, then stooped and lifted the collie onto the seat.

'He can go in the back,' I said. 'I don't mind.' But he shook his head and climbed into the passenger seat with the collie between us. I heard Lop, who was in the back, make a sound of surprise; he is never allowed on the front seats.

We talked on the way about the weather and the crops. As I stopped at the old man's door, I thought to ask him whether he'd seen any signs of a man living rough.

He paused with the door open and one foot outside. 'The police was asking me the same thing,' he said. 'I still keep an eye on things about the farm. It's my son's business now but I notice wee changes. About a month back, I saw that some greens had been pulled, and I telled them that. After that, maybe a week or so since, I was out of my bed one night wi' the neuralgia and I looked outside. Around three in the morning it was. And in the moonlight I saw a mannie walking across the field.'

'Did he have a full set of whiskers?'

'Aye. That's how I kenned that he wasn't from around here. There's nobody at this gate-end could grow whiskers like that.'

'Was he carrying anything?'

'He was habbling, right enough, and he looked humpy-backit. It was next day I found some neips was gone from my clamp. I jalouse he had a sack over his shoulder.'

If the figure was laden it was a safe bet that he was on the way home. 'Which way was he heading?' I asked.

The old man jerked a thumb in the general direction of the moor, whistled his collie to jump carefully down and the two of them set off along the path.

Wal, Keith's partner, had been giving a client some lessons in casting one evening on some water below our beat of the river and he reported seeing fresh-run salmon making their way upstream. If the early spring run of salmon up north was being repeated here, it would have been folly to ignore the unusual bounty. An evening of fishing could be worthwhile. There were no visitors just then and Sir Peter was away, but Deborah decided to join me. She doesn't usually bother much with fishing although she can cast a pretty line.

Well, thank you. In fact, I knew by then that I

51

was pregnant but I had not told anybody, especially Ian. I knew that Ian would be convinced that the kick of a shotgun could be enough to make me miscarry and he would want to wrap me in cotton wool and put me away in a drawer until it was all over. Solicitude can be gratifying but it is also a dead bore. So I had made up my mind to get what sport I could while I felt fit and agile and could still get into my chest waders.

Sir Peter had me chasing around putting out Larsen traps for the magpies which had suddenly appeared in plague numbers, so it was afternoon before we got down to the river in my Land-Rover. I left Lop at home. He never really took to the fishing.

We donned our waders in the bothy and I set up both rods. I only had one buoyancy aid available, an inflatable lifejacket, and I made Deborah put it on and blow some air into it. I know every stone in the riverbed, but she has done most of her fishing with Wallace on the Tweed.

We walked softly to the top pool and took to the water. The river was high and there was a fast stream running. I let Deborah start a hundred yards ahead of me and began casting. Deborah hooked and landed a fish after a disappointing fight and I had a good pull but lost him. After that it went quiet.

When the light began to fade, we were both near the bothy. Sea-trout rest deep down by day and often move on upriver after dark. It was too early in the year for a run of sea-trout but it is in the nature of fishermen to be optimistic. If the salmon could arrive early the sea-trout might do the same.

We decided to fish on. I boiled the kettle and made tea while Deborah changed our flies for bigger lures – her fingers are smaller and nimbler than mine and her eyes are sharper.

It was almost pitch dark when we resumed. There was just a faint glow from the moon above heavy clouds, enough to show the outlines of the bankside trees and give a reflection from the water. Deborah went off downstream, bypassing a rapid glide, and I started again where I had left off, just upstream of the bothy.

I had the sound of the bustling river in my ears and the wind was sighing in the branches above, almost covering the stealthy sound; but my night vision had come back and I could just make out a dark figure by the bothy. He must have known that I was there – there is no mistaking the sing of a rod and line. If I reeled in, he would hear the ratchet working and know that I had changed my rhythm. I edged nearer to the bank, made one more cast and then wedged my rod upright into a patch of reeds. My wading staff, with the net screwed into the top of it, I pushed onto the bank which was at least chest high at that point.

I started to climb out, but when I was halfway up and standing on a projecting root which I had used many times before, I saw that the dark shadow had come closer. I pulled out my torch. It was only a small torch, useful for changing a fly at night, but after the darkness it seemed as bright as day.

It was the same wild figure that had charged at us on the moor, but this time he was standing still, six feet away, with a gas cylinder in each of his hands. I would never have recognized him behind those whiskers but there was something familiar about his eyes.

'Is that you, Dougie?' I said.

'Never you bloody mind who it is,' he said harshly. I recognized his voice although he sounded clumsy, as though he had become unused to using his tongue. 'Don't come up any higher or I'll brain you with one of these.'

Not wanting a gas cylinder on the head I stayed where I was, but I still had a message to get across. 'You can help yourself to rabbits and pigeon and welcome,' I said, 'but if you make an inroad into the game-birds I'll come after you. And a fish or two wouldn't bother us, but if you net a pool I'll know and I'll pull you like a wishbone.'

'I only came to change my gas cylinders,' he said quite mildly, for all the world as if he was in the ironmonger's shop, and he added, 'I could use a few fishhooks,' in a wheedling sort of tone.

Sir Peter wouldn't be too bothered about the cost of changing the cylinders a little oftener than usual, so I let it go by. I had had an idea. There's no keeper like a reformed poacher. 'For every fox you can kill,' I said, 'you can take a pheasant and I won't bother you.'

'Including cubs?'

'Including cubs,' I confirmed. A cub today may be a vixen with her own litter to feed next year. 'Why did you leave the four-ten in the heather?'

'Found it, did you? Because I sprained my ankle in the darkness just after I hurdled that dyke,' he said. 'That's bloody why. It was all I could do to get back to—' He stopped.

'Yes? Dougie, where the hell are you living?'

54

'Where you won't find me. Nor the police. I've seen them poking around. By the time I was fit to hobble back to the moor, you'd gone ahead with the muirburn.'

'Hamish got shot in the knee when the cartridges went off,' I told him.

'Tough! Tell him to take more care next time. Tight lines,' he added – a fisherman's farewell. I had put the torch away to save the battery but I saw his outline stoop, to change his grip on the cylinders, I thought.

'Hold on,' I said. 'You were there when Nat left home, just before he died. Tell me what really happened.'

Dougie straightened up slowly. 'Nothing much to tell. You said most of it. I was with them in the room, me and the housekeeper body, waiting for orders. He got a message. He rushed away. He hit a tree.'

Standing awkwardly balanced on the tree root with the river pulling at me was giving me cramps in my legs but I had questions to ask anyway. 'Could somebody have tampered with his brakes?'

'No way.'

'You couldn't have been watching it all the day.'

'I wasn't,' Dougie said. 'But if there'd been anything wrong with his brakes, he wouldn't've got away along the road. He'd've crossed the road at the end of the drive and hit the bank on the far side.'

That seemed to settle that. 'Did he say anything before he left?' I asked.

'He got a phone call. He turned white and said that it was too soon, that he wasn't ready, but he couldn't hang on or it would all be up. Up what, he didn't say. He ran downstairs and I heard his feet on the gravel. Madam went to the window and called down, something about money. That's what you want to know about, isn't it, the money?'

'I'm curious,' I said.

'I bet you are. You and every bugger. He shouted something back, but if I heard it right I couldn't make head nor tail of it. Enjoy your fishing.'

He stooped again, picked up my wading staff and pushed me hard in the chest with it. I fell backwards into the water.

God, but it was cold! I hadn't been feeling it before. My insulated waders had been saving me but they were as likely to be the end of me now. As my waders filled, the last thing I needed was trapped air rushing down into the boots. I stayed on my back, spread my arms and bent my knees. The current swept me along close to the bank, but I had time to think that my lure would be well down on the stones by now so that I'd have to be unlucky to get the hooks into me.

I felt and heard the water speed up as I entered the glide where the river fell to the lower pool. I took a deep breath. My chance to crawl out might come at the boulders and shingle bank further down. But my head hit a rock, the current rolled me over and by the time I was swept into gentler water I was out in midstream where the water was ten feet deep and I knew for a fact that I was going to drown. An angler had drowned at the same place few years earlier. I had lost the air in my lungs, my clothes and waders were dragging me down and only the frantic paddling of my hands was keeping my head mostly above the surface.

I don't know what fool said that a drowning man's whole life flashes before his eyes. He must have been daft. Anyway, how would he know? The only thought in my mind was that, if I managed to live and ever caught up with Dougie again, I would give him a kick up the bum that would split him right up the middle.

Deborah saved me and as long as I live I'll forget her impudence and be grateful for it. It was dark there, under trees, and how she knew what had happened or where I was I'll never know, but I felt something slide over me and then a stab as she sank two hooks of a treble into my shoulder.

I had heard voices up by the bothy and I was trying to listen. Then I heard a roar and a mighty splashing. There was no doubt that somebody had fallen in and, from the language, it had to be my uncle. The water was dark but the slope of the glide was reflecting a little light and I saw a dark shape come down. I had just recovered my line and it was easy enough to cast over the place where all the swearing was coming from. Once I had him fairly hooked it was just a matter of pulling as hard as I dared without risk of breaking my sixteen-pound leader or pulling the hooks out of his hide and clothing. The current helped me to swing him into the shallows.

I had a torch of my own and I shone it on him. He crawled out of the water like some hideous monster. He was a mess, a deep gash in his scalp, more blood from where my hooks had almost torn out of his shoulder and between his coughing and spluttering he was still swearing so hard that it was

57

a wonder that the now absent Dougie didn't spontaneously combust.

But he was alive. The first thing he did was to cut my line away from the hooks in his shoulder. Next he lay on his back with his legs in the air to drain the water out of his waders. Then he produced a pair of pliers which I gathered he keeps for the purpose and nipped off the barbs and points so that he could withdraw the hooks. After that – would you believe? – the old bastard was game to go back to fishing.

We decided to pack it in for the night. Although I told her there was no need, Deborah insisted on driving me up to the hospital where they put stitches in a cut that could have healed without them and gave me injections to prevent me catching anything, from anthrax to Weil's disease.

For a while, I wondered whether Dougie would remember and respect our bargain, but I was not left to wonder for long. Ten days later, when the lump on my head had gone down and I could straighten my back without wincing, I found a dead vixen and her four young cubs on my doorstep in the morning and over the next few days five neat little piles of cock pheasant feathers appeared, always in the middle of a track I used regularly. Which, Sir Peter agreed, was fair enough. Each fox would have accounted for far more than one game-bird and we had enough wild cocks to serve all the hens. A surplus of cocks on the ground during the spring and summer is more of a damn nuisance than a blessing and Dougie knew it as well as I did. A packet of mixed fishhooks vanished from the window sill of the bothy.

After that, there was no sign of Dougie apart from my coming across the occasional snare. He left the bothy alone although I heard of a visiting caravanner, come early for the fishing, who went to the ironmonger in a rush because he'd been caught out by empty gas cylinders when they should have been full. He wanted a rebate because the valves must have been faulty but he didn't get it. Sir Peter, who is very much a fly-only man, hooked and landed a large trout in the small loch that he owns and keeps for his own use. The fish had in its jaw a rusting, long-shank hook which had never been the basis for a fly. Somebody had been fishing with bait, probably worms. But, of course, it might only have been boys.

I was still going to give Dougie that good kick up the backside for the ducking he'd given me, but it looked as if that day was a long way off. In the meantime it seemed that we had some kind of an unwritten understanding. I was still busy. I forgot all about the rogue for the moment until a chance meeting brought him back to mind.

Winter lingers late, this far north, and spring arrives in its own time. The first flowers were out, the trees were beginning to bud and we were having one of those summery days that fool you into leaving off your semmit ready to be caught out by the next late blizzard. I had more or less caught up with my work and Hamish's too. Hamish was hobbling around. He was driving, after a fashion, but still not very mobile on foot. He couldn't carry a sack of

59

pheasant crumbs but at least he could limp round a line of traps.

It was time and weather for some rest and recreation. One evening, I picked up Hamish in the Land-Rover and we went to the Canal Bar. This is neither one of your flashy modern bars with plastic tables and plastic barmaids nor pompous and up-market like the Newton Lauder Hotel, but a good old-fashioned pub with pitch pine linings on the walls, waxcloth (*he means linoleum*) on the floors, no jukebox and the drinks at prices which, as things go today, are almost reasonable. A man can feel at home there.

We were on our second pints and talking about the fishing prospects – there had been little snow that winter to keep the rivers filled – when I heard a woman's voice calling my name. I looked around. At a table half hidden from me by a group of men in front of the dartboard were two ladies, both of them in their middle thirties at a guess. One of them, a homely looking body but with a twinkle in her eye, I had never seen before but I had no difficulty recognizing the other. I had not seen Mary Milburn for a ten years at least, but she had been a beauty in her day and she had worn well. There had been a time when we were close friends.

Close? Friends? This is an understatement of the first water. I had only just entered my teens at the time, but my uncle's affair with Mary Milburn had been enough of a local scandal to force itself on my notice if not my understanding. It was whispered that they had once had it away in the back pew of

a church during morning service although the story,
if not apocryphal, by the time it reached me was no
doubt greatly exaggerated. My uncle was never
much of a church-goer.

I tried to draw Hamish into making up a four-
some, but his knee was hurting him and he asked
to be excused. The other lady, who Mary introduced
as her widowed sister-in-law, said that she'd have to
be going before her niece, who was baby-sitting, got
fed up. She was the driver and she offered Hamish
a lift provided that I'd see to it that Mary got home.

The reader will note that there is no mention as
to whose home.

Mary was drinking vodka and tonic, so I decided
to have a dram. 'You disappeared all of a sudden.
What have you been doing with yourself all these
years?' I asked her. I thought of asking her whether
it had been something I'd said, but I decided that I
had better not, in case it had.

'Married,' she said. 'And widowed. He was a good
man, but not strong. We never had any family. And
yourself? Did you ever marry?'

I shook my head. 'I never quite got over losing
you,' I told her. A little sweet talk never goes amiss.

She spluttered with laughter. 'I haven't been too
far away to get news of you. The last I heard, you
had a Polish ballerina living with you. It was the
talk of the town.'

I decided to get away from that subject in a hurry.

Women never like to hear about other women. Besides, my year with Butch had been something special, the happiest in my life. She's back in Poland now but I get a card from time to time and a bottle of vodka at Christmas. Damn, I still miss her! 'What brings you back to these parts?' I asked Mary.

'I've not been far away,' she said. 'I told you. I was housekeeping for a lady, but she's a widow now and she can't afford my wages any longer. Husbands don't seem to wear well around here. I'm staying with Maisie until I find another place.'

'That won't take long. You were always a grand cook.'

We chatted away about old times – who had made good, who was in the jail and who had gone into politics and was likely to join them. I'll say this much for myself, I've never parted from a lady other than as friends and there's not one of them isn't ready for a chat when we meet and even a cuddle if there's not a husband in the house at the time. Mary bought a round and I bought another and so it went on and before we knew it closing time was on us.

'Do you drive?' I asked her.

'Aye, I do. But not when I've had this many.'

'Nor me. We'll leave the Land-Rover here and go to my place. It's an easy walk.'

She stood up and wobbled. 'It'll need to be,' she said, but with an arm round each other to steady us we made it home. Lop must have remembered Mary although he had been a young pup when he last saw her. Like me he can sometimes show a scratchy and unwelcoming side of himself, but he was all over Mary.

It was as if the years had never come between us.

In the morning when I was ready to leave for my work, she came into the kitchen wearing one of my shirts as a nightie. I showed her where all the makings for breakfast were kept. 'Will you still be here when I come home?' I asked.

'If you want me to,' she said. 'Maisie will be glad of the room.'

'I want you to,' I told her. Damn, but she was still a fine-looking woman! These days, you can't buy shirts with a decent length of tail on them and she had the prettiest backside I ever saw, ready to bleed juice like a peach if you bit it. 'By the bye,' I added, 'I still don't know your married name.'

'Jablinska,' she said. 'His dad was a Pole left over from the war.'

The name rang a bell very faintly but it was half-way through the afternoon before I made the connection.

She was there when I came back in out of the fresh rain. Her clothes had been fetched and some of her ornaments were on display. The place had been tidied and things moved to where she thought they looked neatest, not where they were handy. Some time I would have to explain that the matches lived on the end of the mantel so that I could reach them from my chair and that my hat stayed beside the door so that I could grab it up when I was going out in a hurry, if I got news of poachers or a wounded deer.

But for the moment it was good to have a woman's things about the place again and a good meal waiting when I got home. Sometimes I thought that maybe I should have got married, but then again I remembered that a wife gets to own a part of you. On the whole I've been happy as one of a pair of individuals, not half a couple nor yet quite on my own. There's a difference. There's a lot of species that choose a mate for life but only come together again each mating season. Maybe mankind was like that once and maybe we should have stayed that way. There's a lot to be said for it.

We did the washing up together and then took to the sofa. It had turned cold enough for a log fire, giving the room a look which to me was cheerful but which she thought of as romantic. Lop, curled up on the hearthrug, smelled of damp old dog but Mary didn't complain. That's a good test of a woman.

Direct questions might have put thoughts into her head. I decided to approach with subtlety. 'Who was the widow you were working for, then?' I asked.

She was darning one of my socks. 'Mrs Connerty, over at Gillespie House,' she said without pausing in her work.

'Connerty? I think I was at school with her husband.' I tried to sound surprised. 'Whatever happened to Nat in the end?'

She hesitated and then decided to be blunt. 'He was killed in a car crash, running away from the police. It was in the papers.'

'I'm not a great reader,' I said, 'but I did hear rumours that he was pulling fast ones with his car businesses.'

She put aside her darning and leaned back against me. 'The rumours were true,' she said. 'A pity! Such a nice couple. He could have got honestly rich if

64

he'd let the business run straight. But him, he had to play games.'

The word 'nice' means different things to different folk. My meaning for it could never have applied to the Nat I knew. 'He was a tricky bastard when he was a loon,' I said.

I felt her sigh. 'I wouldn't have trusted him an inch,' she said, 'but he had good manners and he was considerate. You can't ask much more of a man. His trouble, I think, was that he had charm – they both had, but he was the one who knew it. He found that he could convince anybody of anything and he just had to go on and on until it all got out of hand. As for her, she could charm the birds out of the trees without trying or even knowing that she was doing it. That's all she was left with – charm, debts and the house – after the crash.'

'She was lucky they left her with the house,' I said.

'She told me why. The debts were Mr Connerty's but the house was hers. He gave it to her in the beginning, when they were first married, and nobody could say that it had been bought with dirty money. His shenanigans came later. It took an awful lot of keeping up but she loves that house. I'll admit it's a lovely place but I wouldn't have it myself, not unless I could have two housemaids and a gardener to help me keep it. She'd made the gardens all by herself, with some help from Dougie Slattery and one of the farm labourers. It would have broken her heart to give it up or let it go to rack and ruin.

'She tried the DHSS, but what she could get from them hardly paid for the paint that was needed. By this time, she was trying to keep the place up on her own, painting windows when they needed it and doing wee jobs of joinery or fixing a gutter, all by herself.

'For a while, some of her old boyfriends helped her out, but she wasn't a young lassie any more and that soon tailed off. If any of them fancied her for a wife, she didn't fancy taking him for a husband and giving up some of her rights in the house.'

Mary broke off. She was too loyal to mention the ladylike whoring with live-in lovers and I respected her for it. Some things don't become dirty until you talk about them, which doesn't say much for the cleanliness of the human mouth.

I got up to fetch a glass of my homebrew for each of us. I may not be a wine maker like Deborah but I do have a touch with beer. Mine goes down like a mild lager but it has a punch. Once, when he and Keith were arguing some point about guns, Sir Peter let me fire his grandfather's elephant gun and it had the same sort of kick. If Mary was in a talkative mood, my homebrew would help her along. She settled against me again. She smelled faintly of soap, no perfume at all. I always did like the smell of an unperfumed woman. Lop was dry now and smelled better. I called him to me and ran the fingers of my spare hand through his coat, feeling for sheep-ticks. He knew what I was doing and kept perfectly still.

'So in the end she had to let you go,' I said.

'That's the way it was,' Mary said sadly. 'It was just a month ago. She said she'd have me back in a minute if things changed for the better and I said I'd come back like a shot. I would, too. She's a real lady.'

'Well, it's all a strange world to me,' I said. My fingers found a sheep-tick and I began to twiddle it round and round, always anticlockwise. That dizzies the tick and also winds its three jaws out of their grip. 'I pay my bills as they come in. I couldn't abide knowing that I had debts hanging over me. Maybe that's why I'll never be rich.'

'You do all right,' Mary said lazily. 'This is a grand wee house.'

I had bought the house with my share of one of Keith's capers and the ladies of the family had done it up for me with the insurance money after the flood. When the canal burst its bank, I mean, not the earlier flood, which was a bit before my time. But there was no point telling her all that.

'Didn't Nat seem fashed while the debts were piling up?' I asked her. 'I'd've been out of my mind with worry.'

'He was dashing about, seeing people. I dare say he was out of his mind with worry, but he was never one to let it show.'

I had the feeling that if I asked too many pointed questions she might dry up, out of loyalty to the lady. The tick came off in my fingers. It was little more than a bag of blood by now. I flicked it into the fire. Lop went back and lay down on the hearth-rug so I knew that there weren't any more ticks making him itch.

While I refilled our glasses and added a log or two to the fire, I chose between several possible lines of approach.

'I've always wondered how the Maxwells of this world manage it,' I said at last. 'Their empires crumbling around them, disaster and disgrace looming ahead and they have to go on smiling and acting as though nothing was wrong, right up to the end.

Then, if they don't go down with a heart attack or top themselves, they face the music, still smiling and denying what everybody knows to be true. Me, I'd have crawled down a hole and pulled it in after me.'

'But he had more guts,' she said. Then she patted my hand. 'No. I don't mean that. If you knew him as a laddie, you'll remember that he always faced the world as if he was right, even if he was wrong. And he was – what do they call it? Something-active.'

'Hyperactive,' I said. 'You're right there. He never seemed to let up.'

'Well, that's just the way he was. If he was more tense than usual, it didn't show – not until the last week.'

'And then?'

She finished her second glass of my homebrew and went on. She was beginning to slur her words a little. 'That last week he was away a lot and when he was at home he seemed to be sitting on hot bricks. We thought he'd been going to see Mr Wincherly, the finance man, but that wasn't right because Mr Wincherly started phoning up over and over. Mr Connerty wouldn't speak to him except to tell him that everything was in hand and not on any account to come near Gillespie House. And I heard him say, "We wouldn't be in this mess if you'd been doing your job." '

'Wow!' I said.

'Yes. But maybe that wasn't fair, because long before – about four or five years earlier, I think – I was waiting at table when they had Mr Wincherly to dinner and he complained that Mr Connerty never asked or took his advice. "Just a blasted book-keeper," he said, "that's all you want me to be, but qualified as an accountant so as to be able to sign the statements." '

Something she had said differed from what somebody else had said. Mary's defence of Mr Wincherly gave me time to think what it was. 'But he did come to Gillespie House,' I said. I stopped and thought about what I was going to say because I preferred not to let her know how much I knew. According to Ian, Mr Wincherly had stated that he had been at the gates of Gillespie House in time to see Nat Connerty drive away. 'He must have done,' I said weakly.

'You'd think so, but he certainly didn't come right to the house,' she said. 'We all knew that something bad was in the wind but we didn't know how bad it was going to be.

'On that last day – God, but it was terrible! He called us into the sitting-room on the first floor, me and Madam and Dougie, who was the chauffeur and handyman. He'd been trying to reach his half-brother, who'd moved in with the Lacy sisters on their smallholding a few miles away, but there was no answer to the phone. Mr Connerty was going to tell us the arrangements he'd made, so he said. But then the phone went and he answered it. I don't know exactly what was said, but when he hung up and turned back to face us he'd changed colour. Honest, Ronnie, he looked like a corpse. That was the first time I'd realized how bad things were. Madam too. She said, "Nat, for God's sake, what's wrong now?"

' "The police are coming," he said. "And it's too

69

soon. I thought I'd have at least another week. Let me think." He ran out of the room. We waited quietly, not knowing what to say.

'He must have been packing, because when he came back he was carrying a small case. He put it down by the door and walked over to the window. You can see miles from that room. "There are cars coming," he said. "I must go. Hang on, hold the fort and I'll be in touch, sooner or later."

'He was out of the room, grabbing up his case as he went, before Madam could get a word in. His car was on the gravel just below. I was too dottled to take in what was happening but she went to the window and I heard his footsteps outside. She called down to him, something about what was she supposed to do for money? He shouted something back, the car door slammed, the engine started and he was away down the east drive as though the devil was after him – as maybe he was. A few minutes later Mr Connerty was dead, although we didn't hear of it for an hour or more.'

She lost interest in telling her tale just then because she was becoming amorous. My homebrew has that effect on them sometimes – maybe I should put it on the market. Anyway, she was nuzzling my neck and making very free—

At this point the manuscript contains another wholesale deletion, but some of the words are legible because my uncle had used a ballpoint of a slightly different colour. On the subject of their passionate interlude he seems to have been quite lyrical. This manuscript shows him to me in new lights, both as a lover and as a poet.

It was an hour later and Mary, rumpled and rosy the way that women can get, had made us a pot of tea before I managed to bring the talk back to where I wanted it. I knew better than to ask any question that would suggest that I was interested in the money.

'What happened after Nat drove away?' I asked.

'Och, it was terrible. The police arrived minutes later and they just would not believe that Mr Connerty was away. They kept on at us but we'd nothing to tell them even if we'd wanted. There was only myself and Mrs Connerty there – Dougie had vanished in Mrs Connerty's car, leaving us to face the music.

'Some while later, while they were still chasing each other through the house looking for Mr Connerty, more police arrived to tell Madam that she was most likely a widow. And next morning, while they were asking their questions and waving search warrants in our faces, although all that Mrs Connerty wanted in the world was a chance to lie down in peace and quiet, there was a message came over the wee radio that one of them was listening to right beside me, to say that a dead man had been found by the old farm road that leads off to the south and they started off all over again and insisted on Madam going along straight away to identify the body.

'She was sure that she couldn't help, or else that it was a cruel trick and it was Mr Connerty's body they were going to show her, and I begged them to give her a rest or to let me call her doctor, but she said that she'd rather go and get it over. But it was Mr Graham that they showed her lying there, all crushed and broken, she told me. Mr Graham had

71

been a friend of theirs although they hadn't seen much of him or Mrs Graham lately. There had been a falling out over money.'

Her last word reminded me that we were getting away from the point. 'But did Mrs Connerty say nothing at all after her husband drove away like that?' I asked her.

She frowned and for a moment I thought that I'd been too direct, but she was only remembering. 'She turned to Dougie, who was beside her at the window. 'What did he say?' she asked him.

' "Damned if I could make it out," Dougie said. 'I thought he said something about a castle, but I could be way off.'

' "But that doesn't make sense," she said. And it never did, not to me.'

FOUR

I racked my brains, trying to think what to do with the idea that Mary had put into my head, and in the end I decided to have a look around on my own. Next morning, I left the Land-Rover on the track that serves a line of grouse butts at the eastern end of the moor and walked the rest of the way through a cold drizzle to the ruins of the castle. I could have driven closer but not without making enough noise to waken the ghosts.

Footpaths left by the passage of beaters, keepers and sheep trailed across the moor, always following the easiest routes; and I followed them, but on dragging feet, for there was a desolate air about the place and I'm as superstitious as the next man.

At first, I thought that I must be wrong. The castle, on its slight hump of ground, was no more than a square of ragged walls and the base of a tower, nowhere more than twenty feet high and in places reduced almost to ground level. Whoever had demolished it more than three hundred years before – the Kerrs, legend had it, when it had been a stronghold of the Hays – had not been playing games. Much of the stone had later been hauled away and used in the construction of farm buildings. Scotland is littered with these half-forgotten souvenirs of a warlike past.

(They talk of the Scottish nation, but for much of her history Scotland was peopled by clans who fought non-stop with each other. I notice that few songs celebrate Scotland as a whole but almost every small place has a song of its own.)

Within the walls, the uneven ground was a mass of weeds, mostly grass and nettles. There were no droppings to suggest that sheep or rabbits had ever penetrated there although in one place the weeds were flattened by the activity of some larger animal. That place offered shelter to a prone man but on a clearer day would give him a view right across the moor. If Dougie sometimes fancied a little daylight or sunshine, this would be the place to take his ease.

It seemed to me that, if I were building a castle as a safe refuge from enemies, I would give it some kind of a cellar for the storage of food and prisoners. I would need a well – the nearest water was half a mile off. But if there had ever been a well or a stairway down from inside the castle, it had been blocked by the fallen stones and become overgrown.

Outside the walls the gorse began, sloping down to meet the heather. The slope was laced with rabbit tracks and studded with rocky outcrops and fallen stonework but I managed to follow the base of the walls all the way round. It was a rough trip although the castle is small. When I was back near where I had started, I paused for a rest and a good think. I had been so sure that there must be a vaulted cellar to the castle, but I had seen no sign of an entrance . . .

While I did my thinking, I had leaned back against

the stonework just where the old walls stood highest. Gradually it came to me that the stonework was warmer than it should have been on such a cheerless day. Immediately, I knew that I had been wrong to think I was wrong, because I'd been right ever since it had occurred to me that there could be a simple reason for the ghostly light that was sometimes to be seen over the castle. On dark nights, the light of a fire shining up a broad chimney onto mist or drizzle or its own smoke might well make a glow in the sky to keep the Nervous Nellies away.

I looked up. There was no smoke to be seen, but a canny man could keep a fire burning for long enough without making smoke in daylight. I thought that I could detect a faint heat-shimmer. I could have climbed up to make sure, but not without making a clatter. And if I had put a turf or a stone over the top of what was left of the chimney, Dougie would have been driven out all right but he'd have been far away before I could get down again. I would have to do it the hard way.

If I were building a castle for my own defence, I would want a bolt-hole in case it did not prove defensive enough. This time, as I went round, I looked outward instead of inward towards the walls. A man could pick his way over any of the outcrops of rock without leaving a sign, but there was one rabbit track that seemed more worn than the others. Either there was a huge warren there or somebody was in the habit of passing that way. The pathway ducked between two gorse bushes and made a bend, but when I knelt down I could see an opening among the rocks, the mouth of a tunnel just large enough for a crawling man.

The cellar might be vacant but I thought not. The only lifestyle I could imagine Dougie adopting would be mostly nocturnal. If he was inside, he might be sleeping – in which case he might be awakened by my arrival to see an intruding figure against the light. I was remembering that twelve-bore cartridges had been stolen as well as four-tens.

I had been so sure that I would track Dougie to his lair that I had come prepared. I had made up a parcel with some of the things I guessed he might have found in short supply – nothing expensive, just tea and salt and needles, fishing line, some more fishhooks and the like – and I left it in the path between the gorse bushes so that my presence would not come as too much of a surprise. Some nylon line, thin as a cobweb, I trailed between the two bushes.

Time was slipping away and I had to go. Two men had rented Sir Peter's beat on the river together with my services as ghillie for the rest of the week. Sir Peter had asked me to see them installed in the hotel and I needed all my time. My going was several times quicker than my coming and even so I only managed to reach the hotel as the clients were parking in the Square.

My intention had been to go back to the castle that night and be lying in wait for Dougie when he returned from his foraging, but the two anglers were on holiday and they meant to enjoy themselves. Nothing would suit them but to get togged up and along to the river straight away. They fished on until darkness. After that we settled in the bothy for a chat, when a whisky bottle appeared. They had a big hamper of food with them, so I made a midnight snack on the new cooker and it seemed that we'd only been swapping tales for a few minutes before the dawn began to show.

The next night was much the same and the one after that and I was almost happy to see them leave on the Saturday. The fishing was terrible but at least they tipped well and left most of the last bottle of the Macallan. I can't do without my sleep the way I once could. When I'd seen them off, with promises to return next year, I scrambled somehow round the keepering jobs that Hamish hadn't been able to manage, fell into my bed and slept right round the clock.

On the Sunday morning, while all the wives were at the kirk and the husbands were telling tall stories in the bars of the various hotels, I visited the castle again. My parcel had vanished and the piece of nylon had been brushed aside. You can hardly feel that stuff let alone see it, but after a search I found it hanging and put it back where it had been.

When I told Mary that I was going out again that night, she was upset. 'I didn't move in here to sleep alone in a cold bed every night,' she told me.

'You weren't alone last night,' I pointed out.

'I might as well have been. Better, in fact. When you snore, the dogs start barking for half a mile around.' She pouted and then let a smile escape, pushed me into a chair and sat down on my lap. 'A woman can do with a little loving now and again,' she said.

'Did you think I hadn't found that out for myself?' I asked her. Dumping herself down on me like that had caught me uncomfortably but it wasn't a good moment to push her away. I had been doing some thinking. 'You can come with me if you like,' I said.

'When we get back, I'll give you all the loving you can be doing with and maybe more.'

She looked at me with one eyebrow up. 'There's an offer to turn a girl's head! Delusions of grandeur now! Where are we going?'

Her weight was bringing the tears to my eyes. 'Hop up a minute and I'll tell you.' She got up. I arranged myself more comfortably and sat her down again. 'I want a word or two with Dougie Slattery.'

I felt her jump. 'That old rascal? Where is he? I thought he'd gone abroad.'

'He's not far away.'

I don't know where she was expecting Dougie to be or how she expected him to be living, but she was going to put on her party frock and I had to explain that Dougie's social life had died the death. Eventually I persuaded her into jeans and several of my dark sweaters, and I'm damned if it wouldn't have been easier to persuade her out of them.

We set off when dusk was becoming dark night. Mary was unhappy at first and miserable later and she protested until I shushed her. The weather was still damp and she was used to the country but not to feeling her way across rough ground without a light. I got her to the castle in the end. It was my first visit right up to the walls in darkness and I could see the faint red glow above where I knew the chimney to be. My nylon thread had gone again, so it was a reasonable guess that Dougie was away from home.

On my hands and knees I followed Dougie's path between the bushes and into the tunnel, with Mary following along behind and bumping my bum with her head whenever I stopped for a moment. All the way, she was grumbling in a loud whisper. After a few feet, about when I guessed that I was under the castle wall, I came to a curtain which seemed to have been made out of somebody's blanket. I listened, but there was no sound; so after a few seconds I pushed the curtain aside, switched on my torch and lowered myself the few feet to the cellar floor.

Dougie was not at home.

The cellar was small for a castle basement – between thirty and forty feet long by twenty across and roofed with a single span of stone vault – but then, it was a small castle.

My first impression was that Dougie must have been damned uncomfortable until I realized that the whole space was warm and dry, thanks to the fire which was smouldering in a huge fireplace at the far end and sending warm flickers of light to vanish in the dark stone.

Mary, climbing down behind me, did not have my experience of bothies and making do and she was even less impressed. 'My God!' she said. 'Has Dougie been living a' this time in such a squalor? I'd sooner be dead.'

'It's not so bad,' I said.

I was still shining my torch around. Any bachelor would have recognized the design philosophy. If you need a something somewhere you put it there; if you don't, you don't bother; and never mind what it looks like. Dougie had furnished his abode largely by picking over the town's rubbish dump, but beneath the rough appearance I began to see order and method. A large drum perched over one side of the fire made sure that Dougie would never be

79

short of hot water. Beside it, a stockpot was sending out savoury smells. A large pile of split logs and peat was neatly stacked on the other side. Around the other walls, Dougie had improvised storage out of old pallets and crates. A crude galley at the fireplace end was crowned by a bottled-gas cooker (from a building site, I heard later) and flanked by the cylinders from the fishing bothy.

The vacant floorspace was mostly covered with pieces of worn and ill-matched carpet and also accommodated half of a large oil drum, cut lengthwise and presumably serving as a bath; a low-level bed, the blankets being tartan car rugs; a comfortable looking but much patched armchair; and, almost at our feet, a hole in the floor beneath which I could hear a stream running.

'It needs a woman's touch,' I said.

Mary snorted. Her years as housekeeper in a good house were against her. 'It's not getting mine,' she said. 'Not with a ten-foot bargepole.'

Dougie's storage units held an amazing collection of gleanings from the dump and loot from cars and elsewhere. I came across a well cared for twelve-bore shotgun, which was a relief, suggesting that Dougie was probably unarmed. He had stocked up well with vegetables, the stockpot simmering beside the fire smelled appetizingly of rabbit stew and there was smoked meat in a large ice-cream tub. He had a transistor radio and even a few books, on subjects reflecting their real owners' tastes rather than Dougie's.

A whole section of storage had been made into a rough and ready wine rack. Dougie, it seemed, had been collecting bottles from the back doors of pubs

– I wondered in passing where the corks had come from. He had been a dab hand at home-made wines in our youth, using the products of gardens and hedgerows, unlike Deborah who buys grape concentrates. The rack was filled with bottled wines in a variety of colours – I recognized the deep purple of blaeberries and I guessed that the pale wine with wired corks was elderflower champagne.

'He's been doing all right for himself,' I said.

Mary was studying the collection. 'His apple and elderberry was always his best,' she said. 'I think this is it. Would he mind if we opened a bottle?'

'He might.' I wanted to catch Dougie on the hop and give him the boot up the backside I'd promised him, just to pay him out, not to be found boozing with a woman in his secret den. 'Take a rest,' I told her. 'Show a bit of leg. I want to give Dougie a surprise.'

'You mean, I'm to be a nice surprise for him?' she said indignantly.

'Enough to keep him off balance until I can pay him back for pushing me into the river. I damn near drowned.' And then, of course, I had to tell her all about my encounter with Dougie by the bothy and try to explain why I hadn't told her about it before. But if she was annoyed at me she was furious with Dougie.

She sniffed suspiciously at the bed and prodded it, but when she was satisfied that it was clean enough and bone dry she lay down. 'You made me put jeans on,' she reminded me.

'Take them off.'

'That I will not!'

I switched off the torch. 'I can hardly see you by the light of the fire,' I said. 'I want Dougie frozen

81

to the spot, just for a few seconds. After that, believe me, he won't be looking at you.'

She hesitated for a little longer, but she was mad at Dougie and, besides, she was always game for a little mischief. She slipped out of the jeans, folded them carefully, laid them aside and pulled my sweater down to make a miniskirt. She gave me a big grin. 'How's this?'

I had added a couple of logs to the fire and the new flames flickered with a soft light that took years off her. 'Bonny,' I told her. 'A real centrefold.' Dougie would have been without any female comforts for a long time. The vision of Mary gleaming out of the dimness should make him pop his cork long enough for me to get my hands on his miserable neck.

I sat myself on a spare oil drum by the mouth of the entrance tunnel, out of the sight of anyone coming in.

As a stalker, I had learned patience long since. I've spent many a long hour waiting for the chance of a stag or watching a fox's earth. But that night the time seemed to grind very slowly on its way. Maybe it was that Mary, in the flattering glow of the firelight, looked younger and more alluring by the minute. I began to wonder if Dougie was coming home at all that night. I think that Mary slept for a while but when, after an hour or more, she said, 'Come and take a rest,' I decided that I might as well be comfortable. I would surely hear Dougie coming. Wishful thinking, perhaps, but that's what I thought. I found an empty tin can, filled it with pebbles and hung it in the passage to be sure.

We must have dozed off, because the first I knew of Dougie's arrival was when he lit the lamp.

My uncle, understandably, has Bowdlerized this part of his story. I got the unexpurgated version from Dougie Slattery on a much later occasion.

'I had my own nylon thread across the path,' Dougie said, 'and when I found it trodden down I knew fine who was waiting for me and why. So the cannie of stones came as no surprise.

'I took it down and went in very quietly, but they'd forgotten all about where they were and who might be creeping up on them. They'd never have noticed if I'd gone in at the head of a pipe band – if the pipers could have played, which I doubt. The pipes are meant to be played on the march, not while the pipers are crawling on their bellies. I could hear the two of them before I was even in the entry passage. They were going at it hammer and tongs. That uncle of yours was bellowing like a stag in rut while Mary was wrapped tightly around him and hooting like an owl.

'My first thought was to pour a bucket of water over them, but my blankets were newly washed and I'd no wish to soak my mattress. Instead, I gathered up their clothes, which were scattered as if they'd blown off a washing line, and tossed them out into the tunnel. You'd think that that uncle of yours at least would have had the sense to keep his breeks on. Then I picked up my gun and a couple of cartridges.

'Mary had her eyes tight shut – for which I couldn't blame her, that uncle of yours is a dreadful sight when his blood's up – and they were still making enough noise to drown any small sounds of mine. I waited until the worst was over, which was considerate of me when you come to think about it. The first they knew of me being there was *when I kindled a stick at the fire and lit the gas lamp that I'd got from a derelict caravan, so that the place was suddenly as bright as day.'*

Dougie paused in his story. Between my hiccups of laughter I was saving up every word for use next time Uncle Ronnie dared to criticize my behaviour, which he does on the least excuse. 'How did they react?' I asked.

He grinned all over his wicked face. 'It was as if I'd touched them up with an electric cattle-prod. Your uncle rolled over and Mary tried to cover herself with her hands – it was only later she thought to burrow under the blankets. I wasn't complaining, you understand; I'd hardly had the sight of a lassie for long enough and she was a fine figure of a woman. Ronnie would have gone for me like a shot, which was why I'd picked up the gun – the sight of it soon cooled him off. "Where the hell's our clothes?" he asked me.

' "You'll maybe get them back if you ask nicely," I said, not letting on that they'd find them anyway on their way out. "If not, you can walk home the way you are. I'll not ask you what you were doing because I ken damn fine what you were doing; but did you have to come all this way to do it, and in my bed?"

'Mary was blinking in the bright light. What with one thing and another, her face was very red. A high colour suited her. "We were waiting for you to come home," she said. "We're just visiting."

' "I hope you weren't bored," I said, as polite as herself.

'Your Uncle Ronnie's curiosity was always practical when he wasn't losing the head. When we

*were lads, he was aye the one who wanted to know
how and why. Now that he was seeing the place lit,
he was looking around him. "Did you hump all this
rubbish up here by yourself?" he asked.*

*At this point, their stories more or less converged
again. I will let my uncle's version stand.*

'You surely didn't carry all this up here on your
back,' I said.

'I used a car.'

'What car? The car you went off in was recovered
in Newcastle.'

'Any car that was left out at night,' he said
impatiently. 'Remember who you're talking to. You
wouldn't expect locks to keep me out, would you?'

I remembered occasions when I had found myself
surprisingly low on fuel. 'My Land-Rover?' I asked.

'Or anything else that wouldn't show the dirt,' he
told me. 'What were you wanting with me?'

'I just wanted to finish our chat,' I said. 'You've
no need to get fretful about it. After all, if I was
going to clype to the police about where you were
hiding out, I'd've done it days ago when I first
tracked you down.'

He nodded. 'I was half expecting it and keeping
an eye open, ready to start running again.'

Living wild like that, he must have developed the
instincts of a fox. As I said earlier, a vixen will
remove herself and her cubs to another den as soon
as she suspects that her present one has been discovered. 'Why didn't you?' I asked.

He looked around him and shrugged. 'Walk into
some hotel, looking like this, and ask for a room?

85

Thanks very much. I'll go on living rough. And where would I find anywhere as couth as this? Anyway, I didn't think you'd tell. You'd be more interested in getting your own back.' He paused. I thought that he looked a bit ashamed. 'I did wait to see that you weren't drowned,' he added.

'Well, bully for you,' I said. 'That makes it all right.'

He sniffed defiantly. 'You'd have done the same, or worse. How did you find me?'

'Mary told me where.'

Dougie gave her a reproachful look and Mary shook her head. 'I never.'

'She did,' I told him. 'I remembered, when we were laddies, you used to chase the other boys away from here. This was your place, you told them. As soon as Mary mentioned the word "castle" I knew where I'd find you.'

'And why would she be talking about castles? She'd never been near the place.'

'She was telling me of the last words she heard Nat say to his wife. Is that why you came here?'

He gave us a scowl to share between us. 'I came here the way you said, because I knew the place and because I was sure no other bugger knew of this cellar.'

'And you haven't even looked for the money?'

'I've looked,' he said angrily. 'Of course I've looked. I'd be bloody daft not to. Nat came here once or twice when we were young. Like Mary, I thought that it might have been "castle" that he said and I couldn't think of any other castle he might have meant. Maybe he said the "cars'll" be worth some money to keep her going. Or maybe he said "arsehole", thinking of you. Did his money never turn up? There was nothing hidden here, so you can get off home and forget about trying to get your greedy hands on it.' Ah, but he was brave while he had his late master's gun in his hands.

There was no easy answer to Dougie's last slander, but Mary jumped in and saved me from saying the wrong thing. 'I was telling Ronnie that the mistress was having a hard time of it. She had to let me go, so she's on her own now, the poor soul, and trying to keep the garden and do repairs to the house and cook for herself, all without a tenth of the money the jobs call for. If we were hoping to find what Mr Connerty meant and where he'd put his money, it was for her sake.'

Dougie cooled down immediately. 'It's a damned shame if she's left without a feather to fly wi',' he said. 'She's a bonny lady, for all she's maybe not just what the minister would wish her to be. But I'm damned if I could help her. If the boss's money didn't dribble away through the business I've no more idea where it went than the next man.'

Now that he was talking it seemed a good idea to keep him going. 'What did happen, that last day?' I asked him.

Dougie shrugged and settled himself into his wreck of an armchair. The shotgun was pointed at the ceiling. I thought that if he got a wee bit more careless, I could jump him. 'Why not?' he asked. 'It'll not help you or me and least of all herself, but I'm not going anywhere just now and you're in no hurry. Mrs Jablinska can remind me if I miss anything out.

'I'd come back from Rotterdam the day before,

but the feel of the house was much the same – as though we were waiting for something and when it came we'd have to move bloody quick. Like a hare when the hounds are coming. But the hounds weren't all that close yet and the boss, though he was tense, seemed certain that he could win through. Yes?'

'That's how he seemed to me,' Mary agreed.

'One moment,' I said. 'You'd just come back from Rotterdam?'

Dougie nodded. 'The night before. I'd been delivering a top of the range Nissan,' he said.

'You brought back cash?'

'Pounds sterling. Mr Connerty aye insisted on that.' Dougie paused and looked at Mary. 'Did that cash not turn up?'

'Not that I know of,' she said. 'The mistress didn't have it; she was broke from the moment he drove off and selling her antiques and the likes of that.'

'Most likely it burned in the car with him.' Dougie shrugged. 'The boss was still hungry for more money. He had a customer for a good Ferrari Four Five Six GT, and he had all the documents from one that had been crushed under a fuel tanker. He wanted me to go off to London or the Midlands straight away if not sooner and find one – any colour, the buyer was British so it would have to be a respray and a hundred per cent ringing job. He must have been sure that he'd have ten days or a fortnight to turn it round.

'I'd been travelling non-stop for thirty-six hours. I can't sleep on ferries; and to move anything as conspicuous as a Ferrari without catching the attention of the fuzz I'd have had to take the big van, and driving empty it was like steering a cow by the tail, so I insisted on a day's break. And it's just as well I did or I'd have arrived back with a stolen Ferrari to find the police in possession. I spent the day pottering about, doing the chores, washing cars and giving Madam a wee hand in the garden.

'Halfway through the afternoon Mr Connerty came off the phone and called us into the sitting-room. As soon as I came in he began to say something, but he hummed and hawed, which wasn't like him. It was as if he was feared that saying it aloud would make it real and I saw that the mistress was looking at him gey sharp. But at last he got to the point. The crash was coming, he said, and nothing he could do would stave it off much longer. "I'll have to go abroad," he said, "or it'll be the jail for me. You too, Dougie," he said. "You ladies have done nothing, you should be able to ride it out until I send for you."

'Madam asked him if what he'd done had been so terrible. "Surely a good lawyer could get you off with a fine and a caution," she said. But he told her that the best lawyer in Scotland couldn't get him off with less than ten years; once they started to look in the right places, the truth would all come out. And he said that he'd rather be free and rich at the other end of the world than a jailbird at home.'

'The mistress was in tears by then,' Mary said. There was a tear in her own eye, remembering.

'Aye, so she was. She asked him how he would keep in touch and he said that he'd write. His letters might be postmarked London, but she could ignore that – they'd be written from abroad and a friend would send them on, because they'd surely keep tabs on her mail.

'He was going to say more but that's when

another phone call came. I knew who it was from before Nat could say a dozen words – there was a detective sergeant, name of Fulson, who'd been in the boss's pocket for years. I'd have known his rumbling voice clean across the room even if Mr Connerty hadn't used his name.

'The boss listened for no more than a few seconds and then he hung up. He was looking as serious as I'd ever seen him. No, more than that, he was both angry and scared.'

'He was shaking,' Mary said.

'Aye. The mistress asked him what was wrong and he said that the police were coming, and before he was ready for them. "I must get packed," he said.'

'I'd forgotten that,' Mary said, 'but you're right. And Mrs Connerty said that she'd come and help but he said no, that he knew what he wanted and where to find it and that anybody else would only muddle him.'

Dougie nodded impatiently. 'So he did. So he did. And off he went. We just waited, not saying much but easy busy with our own thoughts. I was thinking that, being just back from abroad as I was and expecting to go again any day, my case was already full with as much as I'd want or could carry.'

Dougie got up, still carrying the shotgun. He added some peats to the fire, very carefully so as not to send a shower of sparks up the chimney though who he expected to be outside to notice them at around four in the morning, and with me inside there with him, I'm damned if I know. He settled back into his chair and took up the story. 'It seemed just minutes before he came back with his bag, and maybe it was – I wasn't watching the clock.

90

He was certainly quick. I was standing by the window, not watching for anything in particular but looking out so as not to have to look at Madam when she wouldn't want to be looked at. She was weeping and she aye hated to be seen looking less than her best. I pointed and he came and stood beside me and saw what I'd just seen. There was a column of light-coloured cars, maybe six or seven, coming along a road that didn't usually see that many in a day. No flashing lights, no klaxons, nothing like that, but there was no doubt what they were.

' "I'll have to get going," he said, or something like it. "Hang on here and I'll get in touch." He'd changed colour. He seemed to be speaking to me so I stayed where I was while he hurried out, grabbing his bag as he went.

'Mrs Connerty came to stand beside me. I could feel her shaking. Below us, the boss was getting into his car. She called to him from the window. "Aren't you leaving me any money?" ' Dougie paused and cocked an eye at me. 'This is the bit that interests you?'

There was no denying that whatever had happened to Nat's money was more interesting than a story that I'd heard before from Mary, so I shrugged.

'I thought as much,' he said. 'Well for all the good it'll do you, or anybody . . . He was just getting into his car and his words came in bits and bobs as he stooped and dropped into the seat and then lifted his feet in. But, for sure, I heard him say "You'd better go to the castle—" and then the car's door slammed and the engine started. He was still speaking though you couldn't make out a word he was saying. He wound the window down and shouted,

"You'll be all right but you'll have to send me some. I'll write and tell you where to phone me – from a call-box, mind." The engine revved and he was away.'

'But you're sure of that much?' I asked.

'Not to swear to.'

'The door slammed on the word "castle",' Mary said, 'so that we really only heard the first bittie. That I do remember, because I thought he'd started to say "car showroom". It was the mistress who put the word castle into our heads, looking round, puzzled, and asking was that what he'd been saying. When she said that, I thought at once that she might be right. What did you think, Dougie?'

'I've told you what I thought,' Dougie said, 'and even that much I didn't think at the time. I was too busy with worries of my own. I'd just realized something. I had a key to Madam's BMW in my pocket, but I'd left my key to the boss's car in his dash wi' all my other keys on the same ring. All my clothes and passports and money was locked in my wee house, the money and passports in a cupboard that I'd built myself and that I'd meant to be proof against all kinds of thieving bastards. I tell you, I can get into any car inside of fifteen seconds, but that cupboard had a steel door and two security locks and the spare keys were at my bank. I could have got into it, but long before I'd managed it there would have been cops looking over my shoulder and cheering me on.

'See, there was the other thing. The boss had said to stay with Madam, but he'd forgotten something. If the police wanted him then they wanted me and all, for car theft, taking and driving away and all the charges that follow on from that. I didn't fancy serving everybody else's time like Harry Fury. I'd have to go, there was nothing else for it, and I'd have to be away before the police reached the gates. I got out fast.'

'And never said goodbye,' Mary murmured.

'There was no time for the likes of that. Already the first cars were near the gates. One of the boss's guns was in the hall –' the gun on his knee lifted for a moment '– so I took it along with me, with the thought in mind that I could sell it later or use it on myself – I was in that sort of a mood. I gathered a few things from my own old car, including the four-ten I'd kept back from a car that went to Hamburg, and headed out the back way, up the old farm road and out, in Madam's BMW. That's how I never knew at the time that the boss had scuppered himself.

'I headed south, thinking as I went. I left the car in the ferry car park – it was Blyth, not Newcastle – got a lift to Newcastle city centre and took another car from there.

'I came here first of all. The excitement seemed to be mostly over, but there was still a Bobby at the front gate and a jam sandwich at the front door, so I drove on past and nobody paid a blind bit of notice.

'I needed a bit of time to think, well out of harm's way. A pal of mine was living near Dublin and running a small transport business. It's easy enough to slip into Ulster and across the border. Before I crossed Scotland, I phoned Madam from a call-box. She was alone in the room but from the way she spoke she thought that there was a tap on her line.

She knew my voice at once but she called me Uncle. She told me the boss was dead and she slipped in a mention that they'd asked a lot of questions about where I might be heading.

'I settled down for most of a year. I'd already guessed that the boss had been saying "castle". Nothing else made sense, and he'd known this place when we were laddies. But I might not have done anything about it except that the Garda came for my friend. He'd been working the whole while for the IRA and I never knew. It was only the devil's own luck that I wasn't taken along with him.

'That gave me a fright and a distaste for the Irish. I got out of Ireland in a hurry. I'd no money saved but I remembered what I'd guessed about the boss saying "castle". Whether that was right or not, I thought that I could lie low here.

'The moment I reached here I could see that the boss had never been near the place, or not in the last thirty years. But I made myself at home and it seemed less hassle to bide quietly where I was, rather than start to run and be harassed to hell a' the damn time.

'I'm comfortable enough. I'm a free man and nobody can give me orders. I miss having a dog, though. My old spaniel died just before the trouble broke.'

'Mike,' Mary said.

'Aye, Mike.' Dougie sighed. 'He was a clever wee bugger. I could put my hands on a pup, but it wouldn't be fair on the dog. I miss the company.' He sighed again and the whiskers twitched. I think that he was trying on an ingratiating smile. 'If you should chance to meet up with a woman who could

94

fancy a life away from the pressures of society, I could make her comfortable.'

'You'd make her miserable,' Mary said. But her eye was roaming around the cellar again and I was sure that she was measuring it up for kitchen fitments in case one of her friends should feel like taking up the offer.

I wanted to follow up the question of what Nat had been trying to say. I could recall one or two Spanish restaurants called the Casa something; and the Scots word carse, meaning a fertile flood-plain, recurs in place-names such as the Carse of Gowrie.

But Mary's attention had pounced on something else. 'If you went out by the farm road,' she said, 'you must have passed the place where that man was found dead the next morning. They reckoned that he'd been lying there all night. He may have been lying there when you went by.'

'What man was this?' Dougie asked. 'Mind, I haven't been getting the papers delivered up here.'

'You've got a radio,' I said.

Dougie glanced at the car radio on a shelf, powered by a car battery on the stone floor beneath. 'I brought the radio from the car I drove here,' he said. 'But with all the rest I had to carry I couldn't manage the battery at that time. After I did get my hands on a battery and howk it up here, I've had to lug it down again and do a swap each time I run out of charge. More trouble than it's worth. I thought of pinching a windcharger from one of the farms, but it'd mean setting it up every night and taking it down again before dawn.'

Dougie would surely have been more than mildly interested in the news at that time. Also, it seemed to me that one or another of the town's car owners had been complaining of a flat battery remarkably often and that the death had held the attention of the media for some weeks. But before I could challenge him, Mary was off again.

'You know the old quarry,' she said.

'There's hundreds,' said Dougie. And it was true. The area lies on a bed of good stone and it was cheaper to quarry stone on the spot than to haul it any great distance. Often a quarry was opened in the slope of a hill and returned to the farmer when the immediate local need was satisfied.

'Beside the farm road above the house,' said Mary, 'about a hundred yards before it comes out on the B-road to Briarsburn.'

That made me sit up. 'Is that where he was?' I asked her. I had been up north at the time and reporting had been so bad that I had been left with the impression that the dead man had been found miles away.

'That's so,' said Mary. 'He'd fallen a matter of forty feet from the top of the quarry, they were saying, but his car was hiding the body. It was the car being there that made Mr McDonald stop his tractor and look around. It was Mr Webster.'

Dougie looked interested, as far as you could tell under all that hair. 'Would that be Daniel Webster? Mr Connerty sent me to him to deliver letters now and again. Lived just outside Briarsburn?'

'I . . . I think so,' Mary said. 'From what it said in the paper, Mr Connerty owed him money. The sheriff decided that he'd jumped out of spite, meaning to cause as much embarrassment as he possibly could.'

'Another dissatisfied customer,' I said.

'He wasn't a customer,' Dougie said. 'I never knew nothing about the boss's customers but I knew him. He was up near the house that morning and I heard the boss use the name. He'd put money into the business, a whole lot of it, and he was girning that he was needing it back awful bad. The boss told him to bugger off, that he'd get his money but that if he came back bothering folk and upsetting Mrs Connerty again he'd shoot him or break his neck.'

'It sounds as if he did break his neck,' I said.

Dougie shook his head. 'Nah,' he said. 'The boss was never out of my sight for more than a minute or two from then until it all went wrong.' He sat quiet for a minute or two and I was on the point of saying that Mary and I would have to be running along when he suddenly said, 'I must be old history by now. Ronnie, could you get me a passport? Any passport, so long as the photo looks a bit like me, with or without the beard?'

'Oh, no!' I said. 'I'm not getting involved in such-like shenanigans. I'm a respectable member of the community. The local detective inspector likely still has your collection of passports. Ask him.'

'You could ask him for me.'

'That's right,' Mary said. 'He could. It's Ronnie's niece's husband you're talking about.'

'Well, there you are, then,' Dougie said, as if that made it all as easy as just having to ask nicely and say 'please'. Perhaps nobody'd ever told him that the police don't work that way.

'I could,' I said, 'if you had something to give in return. Otherwise he'd just use me to get his hands on you. You may not be wanted much, but you're still wanted.'

'I might have something to exchange,' Dougie said. 'How would he like to know some more about who was at the quarry?'

'I think he'd be fine pleased,' I said.

'When I went by,' Dougie said solemnly, 'I was in a hurry but not in so much hurry that I couldn't see what was in the quarry. There were two cars there, not just the one.'

'What sort of cars?'

'That's for your DI to get if he coughs up any one of my passports.'

'You wouldn't remember anyway, not after this time,' I said.

Dougie was stung. 'If there's one thing I remember, it's cars,' he said. 'I'm a professional. Leastways, I was. What's more, I knew the car. You ask your niece's detective inspector husband what he'd give to ken whose car was at the quarry at the same time as Mr Graham's. Just you ask him.'

'What shall I tell him you're asking for?'

'Tell him . . . Damn it, Ronnie, tell him I'll give him the lot if he'll drop charges against me. Try it. But if that's too much, see if he'll lower them to where I won't get more than six months, less time off.'

That was about the end of it. We went home soon after.

Once again, my uncle has glossed over a part of the story which shows him as less than a 'respectable member of the community' – Lord save us!

In Dougie's own words, 'When they were wanting away home they asked for their clothes again and for a while I let them sit there, wrapped in a blanket apiece and your uncle cursing like a minister that's fallen down the pulpit steps, while I kidded them that I'd dropped their clothes down the well and that I was going to send them away bare-arsed. They didn't know that their things were in the tunnel waiting for them. Ronnie would have rushed me except that I still had the gun on him. I wouldn't have shot him but I'd certainly have swatted him with the butt. In the end I told Mary that she could have her clothes back if she could pass a small test. I told her to clasp her hands behind her back and hop to the doorway. She wasn't pleased but I reminded her that the longer she left it the more people would be about. In the end, she did it. She made me promise not to watch but she was kidding herself. Remember, I'd been out of the company of the ladies for a long while.

'"What about me?" Ronnie asks. "Do I have to hop?"

'"I'd rather you didn't," I told him. "You don't have the same sort of a bounce as Mary."'

FIVE

The next evening, I paid a call on Ian when I knew that Deborah would be out of the house. I found him struggling with some do-it-yourself shelving. Deborah, it seemed, looks on DIY as a natural outlet for a man's creativity but Ian, who is all thumbs, said that it was his idea of hell. Frankly, Deborah could have done the job better and much more quickly.

Ian seemed glad of a bit of company and an excuse to knock off. He gave me a dram and a tin of beer and took a beer himself and we talked of one thing and another. It was some while before I got around to Dougie.

When I told him that I'd tracked Dougie to his lair, Ian grinned all over his face. He was a dashed sight less pleased when I wouldn't tell him where it was, and when I relayed Dougie's offer of help in exchange for a pardon for his past sins I thought that he'd fly into a tirrivee.

'How about a passport, then?' I asked.

Ian looked angry enough to bite me in the leg and when he bent forward to pick up a dropped beer-mat that's what I thought he was going to do. But he cooled down in a minute or two. 'And what good would a passport be to him without his fare?' he asked.

'You'd have to ask him that,' I said. 'Maybe he's got something he can sell.'

Ian gave me the look that policemen always give to members of the public who try to lead them up the garden path. 'He damn soon would have,' he said. 'If your old school chum only wanted to get his carcass abroad he could go on a day trip and not come back. That way he wouldn't need a passport. But that way he'd arrive in a foreign country without money and, more important, without an identity. To make a living in any country, honestly or dishonestly, you need some sort of identity to produce. What he has in mind is to steal another car, sell whatever's in it to finance his tickets and be in Hamburg or Rotterdam, offering the car to his old contacts, the same night.'

'Very likely.'

'Well, I'm having no part of it. How could I, in all conscience?'

'You'd have to put that to him yourself,' I said.

'I will. Where is he?'

I shook my head and finished my dram quickly before he could ask for it back. I knew I wouldn't get another one even if I hadn't angered him – Ian's much too conscious of the value of money.

He's much too conscious of the value of the Breathalyser, but my uncle is determined to think what he regards as the worst.

'Lend me one of your wee radios,' I said. 'I'll have

101

him talk to you. And no tricks with radio-location, mind.' I've seen what these electronic lads can do with a few bits of wire and some transistors.

'Take him to a call-box.'

'He wouldn't trust you not to have the call traced. And no more would I. You don't want to know about the other car, then?'

'Very much.' Ian scratched his neck and gazed at the ceiling while he thought about it. 'You realize that you're obstructing the police? And harbouring a known felon?'

'Me? What did I say? I called in for a chat about the weather.'

Ian thought some more. From his expression I gathered that he'd taken a scunner to me. (*My uncle means a dislike.*) 'All right,' he said at last. 'I'm not going to connive at more car thefts, not in this country. But I never did believe the suicide verdict. The sheriff likened those marks to the tentative cuts made by somebody preparing to cut his own throat but they looked more like the marks of a struggle to me.

'I'll have to get the approval of the bosses upstairs. Assuming that they agree, here's what I'll do. If your friend Dougie Slattery makes a written statement giving me details of the second car, I will personally drive him to Turnhouse Airport, give him the least illegitimate of his passports, buy him a one-way ticket and put him on a plane to wherever he chooses in Europe. And if he ever shows his face around these parts again I'll have him behind bars before he can blink.'

'I don't think he'll go for it,' I said. 'I'm damned if I would, landing penniless in some foreign airport. Instead, why don't you take him to the ferry ter-

102

minal at Hull, buy him a ticket and put him aboard, complete with passport. He goes aboard as a pedestrian. If he drives off at the other end, that's no skin off your nose. The first thing he'd do would be to pinch a car anyway, so what's the difference?'

'The difference would be between me letting him escape abroad – which is bad enough and would require a vow of secrecy from everybody in the know – as against inviting him to steal a car along the way. Even in exchange for valuable information, it's too much.'

'It does happen,' I reminded him.

'Not through me,' he said grittily. 'He must have stolen or transported hundreds of stolen vehicles in his day. I can't promise to get him off with a reduced sentence but I would promise to try. Or I'll put him on a plane. And that's it.'

'He won't like it. But I'll tell him.'

I wrote a note to Dougie that evening. When I went to the castle the next day, it was too misty for anyone to see me from a distance and I made damn sure that I wasn't followed. Dougie was out so I left the note at the mouth of the tunnel. I couldn't see Dougie swapping his secure home and a life as a loner that suited him fine, for the pleasure of starting from scratch, penniless, in some foreign country, where his knowledge of the language would be limited to a few technical terms and some others of use only in bars and brothels, or serving time in Britain and taking his chance on just how much time he might get. When there was no answer from him after several days, I knew that I was right.

Ian had not lost interest in the matter, not by a mile. He hoped that I'd lead him to Dougie. Not that he was so clumsy as to have me followed directly even if he could have spared the men to do it or found men practised enough in country ways to track a tracker, but wherever I went there was a better than fifty-fifty chance that somewhere along the route I'd cross with a Panda car and see a cop talking to his own fist.

It didn't do them a damn bit of good and it gave us a lot of extra walking because I daren't take the Land-Rover along to the pub any more. Mary complained that her shoes hurt her; and with my job I didn't need the exercise, so we took to staying at home a lot in the evenings in front of a log fire, drinking my homebrew and not being a damn bit bored.

After two weeks, Ian suddenly searched me out. I was on the moor at the time, putting out some grit for the grouse and not very far from the castle, but this time he wasn't interested in Dougie or corpses in quarries. There had been a serious poaching incident some miles off and he wanted me along. He's a clever lad is Ian and he's getting to know his way around the countryside, but it takes a special sort of experience to deal with a poacher.

Ian drove us in a police Discovery. By George, Land-Rover have come a long way since they made my old rattletrap! As we went along, he outlined what little he knew about the matter. It seemed that the estate keeper, a man I knew well, had heard a shot from the woodland edge and had surprised a man engaged in gralloching a roebuck. It was still the close season so he knew that it could not be either of the locals who had permission to stalk there.

These days, a man is wise to approach poachers with great care. Too often they may be members of a commercial gang, not feared to attack a keeper or stalker and not caring much whether he lives or dies – there would be plenty of mates around to swear to an alibi. But this man seemed to be on his own, and professional deer poachers more often go after red deer rather than the much smaller roe, so the stalker went straight towards him ... and the poacher ups with a rifle and puts a bullet through him. Through the shoulder above the lung, luckily, and missing the main artery or he might never have lived to tell the tale.

After about twenty miles we found the place, just where the mixed farmland turns into the barren moorland of the central Borders. The farmer who had gone to the aid of the wounded keeper guided us to a spot from which we could see the local Bobby standing guard over the place where the attack had happened.

The poacher had left behind the roe carcass, which was stupid of him. He may have felt the need to get far away from the place before he was seen again, and without the compromising presence of the roe-buck. But without that carcass there would have been very little evidence for us to find.

It takes an incident such as this one to wake the police up to the fact that poaching is in fact armed robbery. Keepers and stalkers, whose responsibility it is to preserve the estate's expensively hoarded resources from those who feel inclined to help themselves, get so little support at times that they have to co-operate with each other to make as sure as may be, not only that poachers are trapped but also that every case coming before the sheriff is as strong as it can be made. And so there is much exchange of information and, at the end of the day, if we don't know the identity of each regular poacher we know so much about his habits that, when he does slip up, we'll get him.

The bullet which hit the stalker had fragmented, making a nasty mess in the process, but by lucky chance the one in the roebuck had held together. There was no exit hole, so I studied its track. The bullet had gone in through the throat.

I looked at the gralloch, which had been removed with surgical neatness, and saw that the bullet had passed all the way through and I dug it out of the carcass near the tail. It was a treble-two such as I use for the foxes myself, which narrowed it down a good bit because most of your poachers go for the two-four-three. In Scotland, you can shoot a roe deer with a treble-two, but if you use it to kill a red deer they've got another charge to throw at you.

He had gone for the heart and hit it instead of trying a high neck shot which is sometimes favoured by the more skilled shots because the beast is less likely to run.

A gralloch is only a set of guts lying on the ground; but the first cut is sometimes as individual as handwriting. Much depends on the shape and sharpness of his knife-blade, whether his technique is to leave the stomach-bag intact at first and whether he wants to keep the skin. I had come across this man's handiwork before and from what I had gleaned in comparing notes with colleagues there was a good bit known about him.

'He lives somewhere down towards Kelso,' I told Ian, 'and he drives a light-coloured van, white or pale grey, probably an Allegro. You can identify the van for sure if you find it, because he has a tiny lamp mounted underneath, just bright enough to let him see the verge and the white line as he crawls the last half-mile to where he plans to leave the van. You'd better take a sample of this beast's blood for comparison. He'll be home and have washed himself by now, but if you can get to him before all his clothes have been laundered there'll be blood on his cuffs. These days they can match it for sure to the individual beast.'

Ian wasted no time in asking how I knew so much about the poacher – that would come later – but got out his little radio and passed the word along. (I heard later that they traced the man and got a conviction largely on the basis of genetic finger-printing of the buck's blood plus the bullet and the spent brass cartridges that I hunted out from among the blaeberries, but that's no part of this story. At least a daft, dangerous bugger was taken out of circulation for a while.)

Uncle Ron's information led to the man being picked up, but if he seems to be suggesting that the conviction was only obtained due to his inspired suggestion, he's coming it. Ian did a course on genetic fingerprinting years earlier. Also, the keeper recovered and picked the man out of an identity parade.

Before we returned to the vehicle Ian asked the constable whether any search had been made for witnesses.

A chilly breeze was blowing across the hill but

107

that wasn't why the man looked uncomfortable. 'The sergeant took a couple of men down to the road with him, sir. They were to stop cars and make enquiries. He said that that was all the men he could spare. I think that mostly they were waiting to see what you said.'

'And how many men I could produce,' Ian said gloomily. 'I'll tell your sergeant that he can withdraw you now. But he'd better get that carcass and the gralloch bagged, sealed, identified and put into cold storage.' We walked on, leaving the constable to admire a dashed fine view of heather and conifers and stand guarding a few square yards of nothing and some dead meat. Ian used his radio to pass the same message to the local station and to issue some very precise instructions about the search for the poacher.

'Just because there's been no fatality, they don't take it seriously,' Ian grumbled as he drove off. 'Their attitude's a century out of date. There'll always be trouble between the poacher and the estate staff, they think, and people will be hurt, and they know where their duties lie but, whether they know it or not, their sympathies are still half with the poacher. They'll look bloody stupid if that keeper dies.' We passed a Panda car at the side of the road. The driver was listening to his police radio and staring blankly into space. 'Look at that! And they'll call it house-to-house enquiries. I'm going to have a word with the local uniformed inspector when I get back to HQ, and it won't be a word he'll like very much.'

'Just you do that,' I said. As far as I'm concerned, the police can fight among themselves and leave me alone until the cows come home.

108

Ian pulled up beside a gate. A small house with a dilapidated air stood well back from the road in a garden which had mostly run to seed. 'Looking down from the hill, this house seemed to be staring back at me,' he said. 'And if the poacher came from where you say, he must have passed here. I'll bet those dimwits never thought to come here and knock. I'm going to find out. Come if you like.'

I decided to go with him. Any poacher who was going around shooting keepers I wanted to see behind bars, but if somebody answered Ian's knock it would then be too late to go galloping up the path to listen in.

The garden was a mixter-maxter. Parts of it had been left to run wild for years although some fine old rhododendrons and apple trees had managed to survive among the weeds. But here and there one piece or another had been dug over at some time for a small crop of vegetables and then left to go wild again. It was as inefficient a way of gardening as you could think of but it made a splendid habitat for birds and butterflies. The time of year for birdsong was beginning and I never heard them in such voice.

Contrasting with the garden and with the outside of the house, the interior, seen through the windows and through the front door when it opened in answer to Ian's knock, looked surprisingly clean and tidy. So also did the woman in the doorway. She was somewhere in her early thirties, round and fresh faced with tidy brown hair and, like Mary, she smelled of nothing but soap.

Ian introduced himself and showed his identification. The woman answered his questions readily. No, there had been no other policemen at the door that day. And no, she had not witnessed any going-on up on the hill – the kitchen was at the back of the house – although she had been aware of police cars going past. But she had been out pegging up some laundry earlier and she had seen the Subaru of Mr McLennan – the unfortunate keeper – go by. And an hour before that, while she was making the beds upstairs, she had seen a light-coloured van go past. It might have been an Allegro, she couldn't be sure, not knowing much about suchlike things. No, she would not know it again. Her sister would have been able to help, having her own car, but she'd left for her work at the poultry farm by then. She might have crossed with the van, though, the woman added helpfully.

Ian nodded. He seemed to have got all the information that was going. Or almost all. 'And you are Mrs . . .?'

'Miss,' she said firmly. 'Miss Lacy. Doris.'

'And your sister?'

'Anne. Also Lacy. We're both single.' She had a slightly roguish eye, that one.

Ian was ready to turn away but the name had rung a little bell with me. 'You've neither of you married,' I said, 'but am I not right in thinking that there's a Mr Bruce Connerty resides here as well?'

She turned a little bit pink and pursed her lips. 'That's true,' she said. 'But he's my sister's man, not mine.'

Ian looked at me with his mouth open for a few seconds before it came back to him that Bruce Connerty was said to have 'moved in with the Lacy

110

sisters'. But he was not going to admit that I had beaten him to it.

Ian would not have risen to being the kingpin of crime detection in our neck of the woods without a certain talent for bluffing it out.

'He's still resident here, is he?' Ian asked. 'What does he do for a living, now that his brother isn't around any more?'

'Whatever's going,' the woman said. 'There's always work for a strong mannie and he's not too proud to work with his hands. He's been a builder's labourer and I don't know what. Just now he's a security guard.'

'Where?'

Miss Lacy hesitated. 'Where my sister works.'

I could not see even a large poultry farm needing a security guard to fend off egg thieves and prevent feather-picking. Gateman and general dogsbody would be more like it. I could see that Ian had the same thought but he let it go. 'I remember you now,' he said lightly, as though indulging in a little social blether. 'You and your sister came to Newton Lauder to make a statement about the death of Mr Graham.'

'What if we did?' she snapped. Then, recognizing the bad impression that her sharpness would have made, she tried a smile. 'It was only because somebody had raised the question of whether Bruce wasn't at Gillespie House that day. Bruce was here the whole of that day, the day his brother and Mr Graham died; I was prepared to swear to it and I

111

said so. I mind he dug over that patch beside where you're standing. And his car was in for servicing. It was the firm's car really and he never did get it back.'

'Thank you,' Ian said. 'You've been very helpful. How far is it to Gillespie House from here?'

'By road? Ten miles or more.' *So put that in your pipe and smoke it*, her tone said.

We returned to the vehicle. I found a good road atlas and was studying it as Ian drove off. As nearly as I could judge, Gillespie House was no more than four or five miles from Skerriden, which was where the Lacy sisters lived. Across country, maybe half an hour's walk.

I started to tell Ian but he cut me short. 'Never mind that just now. Where's that poultry farm? We'd better find out whether either the other Miss Lacy or Bruce Connerty remembers seeing any vehicles this morning. They won't, of course.'

And they didn't. We found the poultry farm beside a road junction a few miles on; row on row of sheds fronted by a brick office building and a boilerhouse. Ian left me sitting in the Land-Rover at the roadside for half an hour with nothing to look at but a very ugly building and a mountain of coke. I had known Bruce Connerty as an occasional drinking partner for a few months some years earlier and it occurred to me that he might speak more readily to me than to Ian. I strolled over to the gatehouse but it was empty. When Ian came back he shook his head wearily. 'And this one says that Bruce is her sister's boyfriend, not hers.'

'Did you ask him?'

'I caught him attending to the boiler. He didn't

remember seeing any vehicles either. But I couldn't exactly ask him which sister he slept with, or neither, or both, now could I? And, if I did and if he answered me, who the hell would care?'

A fresh run of salmon started up north and again I was sent away up to Sir Peter's other place to ghillie for visiting fishermen. Mary wanted to come with me, but I explained that the bothy I'd be sleeping in would hardly be fit for one of her refinement and that I would be well enough fed by the cook at the Big House.

I bet that he didn't also explain that her presence would have cramped his style with the visiting anglers' wives. See my earlier comment.

It was more than two weeks before I could get south again and the countryside, rightly or wrongly, had made up its mind that spring really was here at last. New colours were appearing wherever you looked and the songbirds were defending their territories. Mary had stayed on in my house and had it all redded and tidied. It looked very bonny but I couldn't find a thing. It took me a week to get it back the way I liked it.

Hamish was back at work and able to do all but the heaviest jobs. That only meant that I could take time off from his jobs to attend to my own and to relieve Keith and Wallace who had been struggling with all the seasonal demands on the shoot that we shared.

Once again, I thought that Ian must be concentrating on current business and forgetting about the old case involving a suicide and a death by accident.

As the days stretched out, I became later and later getting home and I could see that Mary was becoming troubled about something. I thought that she was probably overdue for an outing and a change of company, so I took her out for a visit to the Canal Bar.

Typical!

Mary stuck to soft drinks, as she sometimes did, so we could have brought the Land-Rover after all. She was quieter than her usual and it was difficult to get a conversation going, but it seemed unnatural to sit silently in a pub. When she nodded distantly to a man, a stranger to me, who had just come in, I saw a chance to introduce a new topic and I asked: 'Who's that?'

'That's Harry Fury,' Mary said. 'He used to work for Mr Connerty.'

I looked again. Mr Fury was stocky with thinning grey hair and the sort of round face that you expect to be cheerful. He looked fed up. 'And got jugged for it,' I said. 'Ask him to join us.'

She looked at me questioningly but I think that she was ready to be glad of another person's company. She gave him a friendly wave and when he turned away from the bar with a half-pint in his fist she beckoned to him to come and take the vacant space at our table. He came over, rather shyly. I got up and turned a chair round for him. He was still in mechanic's overalls, I noticed. 'Hullo, Mary,' he said.

114

'Harry!' she said. 'This is Ronnie. My man,' she added in explanation. We shook hands. His was as rough as mine. 'It's good to see you again, Harry. You're working?'

'Ledbetter took me on. Nobody else would. He knew my background but he said he'd give me a chance.' He blinked several times. 'I've been with him two years now, almost since I came out. I won't let him down.'

'And your family?' Mary asked.

'They're fine. You wouldn't know the kids now. I hardly knew them myself when I saw them again.'

Usually it is considered bad manners to refer to somebody's prison record but in this case the subject seemed to be out in the open. 'You had a raw deal,' I said.

I thought that he was going to say that he didn't want to talk about it, but in the end he combined a shrug with a nod.

'But Mr Connerty did go on paying your wages to your wife while you were ... away,' Mary said reproachfully. 'He didn't have to do that.'

'You're still loyal to him?' Harry asked.

Mary thought about that. 'Not really,' she said. 'I know that he had more than his share of faults. But he had his good side too. I was sorry when he died, and not just for his wife's sake.'

Harry looked her in the eye. 'When I heard how he'd died, I was sorry. But it was for the sake of the car, not him. That car deserved a better end. The man was dog-shit. Dog-shit!'

They had forgotten that I was there, which suited me.

'He did go on—' Mary began.

'Paying my wages. I ken that. He could hardly do less. There was a time when I was young and stupid. That's when he put me in as foreman in a new garage he as starting. He was going to pay me well, so he encouraged me to move and buy a house near by. Helped me to get a mortgage. And I was grateful!'

He picked up his glass. His hand was shaking so that the liquid in it danced. He seemed to be speaking in spite of himself and I guessed that Mary's was the first sympathetic ear that he'd found. 'When the family was settled, then it began. Small things at first. Bodging up instead of a proper repair. Giving an MOT and turning a blind eye to a bent chassis. When I objected, he said that the business was unprofitable and he'd have to close it down and make me redundant. So I went on, and soon it was all happening. All the rackets.

'When the shit hit the fan, he sent a lawyer to blow in my lug. I'd done the jobs and nobody could get me off, but they'd put up the best defence they could and my family would be looked after, as long as I refused to say a word about anybody else. Otherwise . . . well, to say they'd be out on the street was the least of it.'

'That was awful,' Mary said, looking aghast. 'I'm sure Madam didn't know.'

'Maybe. But that's not the worst of it. I was a good boy, inside, and I was let out after nine months. On the very day that I came out, he met me. He couldn't employ me again, he said. It would look too bad. Well, I'd half expected that. But he'd taken over my mortgage. And he said that I'd cost him money. I said that I could pay him back if he helped

116

me find another job, but he said I could pay him quicker than that. My house was his, now, and I could move out. And if I tried to make any trouble, he'd swear that I'd come to him to try and extort money. That was your Mr Connerty. Connerty! The Con-artist, we used to call him, and we were right. I'll tell you this, Mary, if Mr Ledbetter hadn't come to my rescue I'd have made away wi' myself.'

Mary shook her head slowly from side to side, whether at the idea of suicide or at Nat Connerty's wickedness I couldn't tell. 'I'm so sorry,' she said.

'You'd no say in it,' Harry muttered. He seemed relieved and yet ashamed at his outburst.

'All the same, I'm ashamed that any employer of mine could treat you so badly and I didn't know; that somebody so wicked could live in the same house and I couldn't recognize him.'

'It was just the nature of the man. I had time to think about it and to look at the men around me in the jail. There are some men that think their manhood's threatened if they leave a sucker with a single penny in his breeks. Your Mr Connerty was one of those and we're well rid of him.'

'But you're all right now?' Mary persisted.

'Aye. The kids have settled well in another school and we're buying another house. It's not as fine a house as the old one, but this time we're not indebted to anyone but the building society.' He looked round. The bar was filling up. He lowered his voice. 'We'd have had to move them anyway. The other kids were giving them a hard time about their old man being in the clink.'

117

Our glasses were empty. I got up to buy a round. Mary stayed with her soft drink. When I returned, Mary was still asking after various aspects of the Furys' new lifestyle but their talk died the death as I gave them the drinks. I decided that it was my chance to get into the conversation.

'Did you do the maintenance on Nat Connerty's Jensen?' I asked.

He nodded. I watched to see whether he relaxed or tensed but he looked much the same. 'He aye brought her to me,' he said. The warmth of the enthusiast was in his voice. 'I kept her running as sweet as you like. Too good for a man as would've been more at home in a Morris Traveller.'

'You reckon that was what killed him?' I asked. 'Just bloody bad driving?'

'What else?'

'I don't know the car,' I said. 'Never rose so high in the world.' I decided to plunge in. 'Would it have been difficult for somebody to tamper with the brakes? Or the steering?'

I heard Mary draw in a quick breath.

Harry Fury looked puzzled rather than angry or guilty. 'It's never difficult to tamper with something,' he said. 'I could well believe that somebody wanted the bastard away. Tampering so that it's not going to fail on the spot nor hold together indefinitely, that'd be definitely tricky.' He paused, frowning, and I judged that he was milling the matter over for the first time. 'And you'd have to be sure that the failure was sudden, so that the driver had no warning. Not easy. Most of the things you could do would start with the brake pedal going soft or play in the steering.'

Mary leaned forward. 'Harry, you didn't . . .?'

'Good God, no!' Harry hesitated and then smiled suddenly. 'Between ourselves, I could have done him in and not lost a minute's sleep over it,' he said, 'but I'd have found another way that didn't mean wrecking a beautiful car. Anyway, I was never at the house that day although I saw him drive away and the car looked all right then. I mean, I'd have noticed if it had been leaking hydraulic fluid or the like of that.'

This was something new. 'You were there?' I asked.

He switched his eyes to me. 'More or less,' he said. 'It was this way. When we'd settled down in the new home, I had time to think. Money was tight, as you'd guess, and although I was glad to be out of it I couldn't help thinking of the big money I'd made when I was ringing cars for His Nibs. I started doing some sums. I added up how much Mr Connerty had paid out in wages while I was inside and it came to a lot less than I'd put down on the house he'd taken off me. So even if you reckoned that he'd a right to do as he did—'

'Which we don't,' Mary said firmly.

'Even so, it seemed to me that I should have had some money coming.

'One Saturday while that was still rankling in my mind, my wife had a fancy to visit her sister who lives not far from Gillespie House, and to let the weans play with their cousins. She'd kept away, you see, all the while that I was inside. While we were there, I decided to grasp the nettle, so to speak. There's a bridle-path through a wood and some fields and I walked it, not enjoying the prettiness of it all but getting up my nerve for what I knew would not be an easy argument. I was used to saying "Yes sir, Mr Connerty," whenever he spoke to me, not arguing with him, and I wondered if I'd be able to stand up to him after all the time.

'The path ended in a second wood just opposite the driveway. I hesitated among the trees, wondering if I mightn't be laying myself open to the sort of accusation he'd threatened and whether it mightn't be better to go through a lawyer.

'I kept up my swithering for too long. I was still there when I saw Mr Connerty, in the Jensen, coming down the drive. He stopped at the road and I saw him look round, and on his face he had the grin that aye came whenever he'd got away with some damned awful piece of real wickedness. He halted a second or two while he took a cigar from his top pocket and lit it with the car's lighter. If I'd had a second longer I'd have stepped out and waved to him, but he was too quick or I was too slow. He moved off, so sharply that another car had to brake.'

I remembered that the financial adviser had testified that he had met Nat in the mouth of the drive. 'Was the other driver going to turn in through the gates?' I asked.

'Whether he was going to or not,' Harry said, 'he didn't do it. The Jensen went out in front of him and turned the other way and then the car drove on.'

Harry offered to buy a round, but Mary said that she'd had enough. Harry said that he'd have to be getting home but I guessed that he was still feeling the shoe pinch. We went out together into a night of drizzle and faint moonlight. Harry drove off in a rusty old Lada.

'Do you really think that somebody killed Mr Connerty?' Mary asked as we walked.

'I'm damn sure of it,' I said.

'But why?'

'Isn't it obvious?'

We walked half the way in silence before she had worked out where we were at cross-purposes. 'I didn' mean why would somebody want to kill him,' she said at last. 'I meant why are you so sure that somebody did it?'

'Damned if I know,' I said. 'I'm just sure.'

As we reached home, Dougie suddenly popped out of the shadows. My guess was that Dougie had been meaning to catch me in Mary's company for the sake of his own health, just as you look for cows in with the bull before going into the field. 'Where the hell have you been, these weeks?' he asked angrily, as though I had to answer to him for my comings and goings. 'And what was yon jailbird saying?'

'I've been up at the place in Sutherland,' I told him. 'If it's any of your business.'

'I could have told you that if you'd cared to ask,' Mary added. 'And whatever Harry Fury was saying, it wasn't about you.'

'And,' I said, 'if he's a jailbird you're a fugitive from justice. At least he's done his time.'

'I don't know who to trust any more.'

'If you couldn't trust either of us,' I pointed out, 'you'd have had the police crawling through your tunnel by now. Are you coming inside?'

I heard Mary's hiss of indrawn breath, too late.

'May as well,' Dougie said.

I led the way inside and while Mary put the kettle on I gave Dougie a dram of my best whisky, the stuff Keith gets through an Excise officer who still owes him for a gun. He rolled the first sip around his mouth and made sounds of enjoyment.

'That's something you'll have been missing,' I suggested.

'Not always. You'd be amazed what men leave in their cars at times. And they don't much fancy going to the police and complaining that a half-full bottle of the hard stuff was taken from the car, for fear that they'll be waved down next time they're driving home from the pub.' He finished his dram in one swallow and looked at me as if to hint that a refill would go down even better. I avoided his eye. There may be certain rules of Borders hospitality, but I still owed him for a ducking in the river.

And worse.

'There's been no word from your niece's husband?' Dougie asked me. 'He isn't ready to deal?'

'I've been away,' I told him. 'I'm only back a few days. But I'd have heard.'

'He's probably thinking that he can get at the truth for himself and then there'll be nothing to stop him going after me and putting me inside for car theft.'

'Looks to me as if he's stopped bothering,' I said.

Mary came through from the kitchen and put down a tray of tea-things. 'Why would Ian waste time worrying over two penn'orth of nothing such as Dougie?' she asked me.

Mary, it would seem, had gone right off Dougie. I wonder why.

Dougie was ready to flare up, but he remembered in time that he was in my house and in need of favours. 'Next time you see him,' he said, 'tell him that I recognized Mr Graham's Citroën Xantia. I got a good look at another car. And I recognized it. You tell him that. And tell him that even if he does manage to pick me up, I'm not saying a word unless I get to walk free with one of my passports. Tell him that as well.'

'All right,' I said, 'I'll tell him.'

Instead of waiting for a cup of tea, Dougie borrowed a whole packet from Mary and faded away with it into the darkness.

'You shouldn't have brought that dirty little scruff inside,' Mary grumbled. 'I washed all the chair covers while you were away.'

That was unfair. Dougie had looked very clean and almost smart in a tweed suit slightly too large for him, obtained, I supposed, from somebody's suitcase left carelessly in the boot of a car. 'He was cleaner than I am,' I said.

'Everybody's cleaner than you are,' she retorted. Then she softened. 'I know. It's your job that's to blame. Anyway, you're all I've got so I'll just have to make the most of you.'

'You sound like you're staying on a lot longer,' I said. On the whole, I was pleased. She was a grand cook. (*This sentence was originally much longer. Such words as remain legible under the heavy deletion seem to be devoted to high praise of Mary's charms as a lover.*)

She poured two mugs of tea and then sat looking at me quietly for a few seconds. Thinking back, I can see that she was wondering if this was the moment. It seems that it was. 'I'll have to,' she said. 'I'm pregnant. We let our affectionate natures run away with us once too often. And I'm a little too old to set out as a single parent.' There was another pause while I sat like an idiot. 'If you're too fashed about it, I could always have it taken away.'

'You're sure? That you're in the road?'

She nodded. 'I bought one of those kits. When it said yes, I went to the doctor. He confirmed it.'

I got to my feet and picked up my mug. 'Wait here,' I said.

I called Lop to me and went out and walked up the road in the moonlight, sipping my mug of tea as I went. A car or two went by, grinding their way up the hill and out onto the open road, but there was a wide verge and Lop was quite safe at heel.

'What do you make of it?' I asked him. He seemed little interested. He'd fathered enough pups in his time that the wonder of it all had gone, if indeed he had ever linked in his mind the deed and the result. But we had always known what the end might be. We had meant to be careful, but all the care in the world may not be enough. Besides that, we had not always been quite sober by nightfall. Well, whatever might be our feelings, there was a part of my life now growing inside her and nobody was going to start snuffing me out. I turned round and went back to the house.

124

Mary looked up as I came in. She was trying to look calm but her muscles were taut. Even so, there was the beginning of that look of fulfilment that women get, now that I knew to look for it.

'There'll be no more talk of an abortion,' I said.

She began to relax. 'I'm glad,' she said. 'I'm getting on. It'll be my last chance.'

'We'll just get married,' I told her. I was surprised that I hadn't thought of it before.

'If I'll have you,' she answered. But she was smiling.

SIX

When the news, which was strictly limited to our engagement, got around, the general feeling seemed to be that it was high time and more that I settled down and that the two of us made our peace with the more respectable members of the establishment. As one friend put it, 'Why should you be happy while the rest of us are married?' It was also assumed that, because we were both coming to marriage rather later in life than was usual, we would not be thinking of starting a family. They had a shock coming.

Our immediate family were kind. Keith shook my hand and forced several drams on me while crying the virtues of the married state and at the same time giving me a long lecture on the best ways to keep a wife contented while still having things your own way. (*I wish I had been a fly on the wall.*) Molly, like any good sister, simply wished me happy (and seemed to mean it) and set about planning a major affair in church. Deborah, the minx, wished us joy of each other and told me, in private, that she was pleased I'd found a woman at last who could make a bed as well as rumple it.

When I had time to consider my own view in the light of fact rather than theory, I realized that I was quite looking forward to the married state. There had been a lot to be said for being single and I had said most of it myself. But being fancy-free means that your partner of the moment is also free to move on, and I had had enough of change and fresh courtships and coming home to cook for myself in a cold and empty house. I'd no wish for a lonely old age, fending for myself while growing less able and always at risk because there would be nobody at hand if I fell or fainted. The idea of a family, a son or daughter to instruct in the ways of nature, began to look very attractive. And Mary . . . There was something about her that made me feel good, and she knew how to turn it on. She was hardly my first love but I thought that she would be my last. That's all there is to say.

And more than enough.

Ian, when I bumped into him, had yet another viewpoint. He led me into the hotel and insisted on buying me a dram while he talked. He was less concerned with our happiness than with his chance of turning it to his advantage. 'This could work out very well,' he said.

'I should bloody well hope so,' I told him.

'Oh, you'll be all right,' he said carelessly. 'Mary will see to that. What I mean is that I've been looking for an excuse to go and talk to Mrs Connerty. She's not been exactly co-operative with the police. Her husband died because he was running away from the police but she seems to think of us as having hounded him to his death.'

'It's all in the point of view,' I told him.

127

'My sergeant tried to sound out her brother-in-law about Connerty's last few days and what visitors had been to the house, but he clammed up immediately. I don't want to make the same mistake with the glamorous widow. I asked Keith to go and see her for me, but he flatly refused to go, alone or with Molly.'

'He has his reasons,' I said. 'So what's changed?'

'This. It's only natural for Mary to want to go and tell her old friend and former employer about her engagement and to introduce her fiancé.'

'Hold on,' I said. 'I've known her as long as Keith has.'

'And as well?'

'Well, no,' I admitted. 'Nothing like.' Jacinthe Connerty, Jacinthe Mathieson as she was then, would never have looked at a roughneck like me. She was a bit above my touch – and I mean touch.

'That's all right then. So you two can call to see her, on the spur of the moment. Just happened to be passing and by chance Deborah and I are in the car with you. Even if she recognizes me as a police officer she'll be more likely to let her hair down if I'm just one of a group of callers.'

'We'll see what Mary says.'

I put it to Mary that evening. I thought that she might have objected to being used as a stalking horse, if that's the right expression; but she trusts Ian and was only too happy to show Mrs Connerty the classier side of the family she was marrying into.

That week, before we could get around to making the visit, Ian caught Deborah sicking up her cornflakes and the secret of that particular pregnancy was out. Immediately, Ian became protective and over-reacted to a few cautionary words from the doctor. There were to be no unnecessary jauntings around, he ruled, and after he'd quoted to Keith and Molly an exaggerated version of what the doctor had told him, they said much the same thing.

There was no need for Ian to put the foot down. I was sick as mud at missing the fun but sicker still whenever my stomach took exception to the little stranger. And petrol fumes seemed to have a special knack of bringing on the heaves. The last thing that I could have endured would have been being bumped around in a smelly car on country roads.

So the idea of taking Deborah along was dropped. But Ian still hoped to pass almost unnoticed in a crowd so Keith was persuaded to make a fourth member of the party on the strict understanding that he was not to be left alone with the widow. I was surprised that he had such a mistrust of the lady but Mary was sure that it was himself who he didn't trust.

In point of fact, Dad didn't trust Mum to trust him except in the presence of witnesses. That's what comes of having a past, as I keep telling Ian.

It was a fine spring day when we set off after an early lunch, the sort of day on which the poet must have written 'It ain't going to rain no more, no more,' because the feeling in the air was that spring would last for ever. The trees were coming into bud and the hedges were filled with blossom. Mary had

129

got me to polish up Keith's car for him (it was the smartest that we had between us) and she'd got me into my best go-to-meetings suit, the one Molly had made me buy for Deborah's wedding after Deborah said that I didn't look quite the thing in a hired morning suit.

What I actually said was that it made him look like the chucker-out in a disreputable night-club.

Mary, of course, was dressed to the nines; in fact, when we called to collect Ian, Deborah made her take off some jewellery and a fancy scarf. She had on the ring I'd bought her. This impressed even me. Keith had used one of his contacts to get me a grand ring at a bargain price.

Unknown to Uncle Ron, Mum had insisted that Dad, as well as screwing a beautiful antique ring out of a dealer who was lusting after a pair of Doune pistols, also subsidized the price of the ring; and she was in the process of persuading him to underwrite a 'proper' wedding as well. In this family, that means white, in church, and not less than two hundred guests in the hotel. I could see Dad having to sell off several duplicates from among his collection of antique guns, but that, as Mum pointed out more than once, was the least he could do for the one member of the family still to take the plunge.

At the junction where Ian and I had turned off

130

for the place where the poacher had struck, we continued, still climbing, on a not very major road to one of the driveways of Gillespie House – the east drive, down which Nat Connerty had raced towards his appointment with the twisted and still blackened oak tree. Mary had pointed it out to us as we went by. The driveway ran between hedges and trees through fields which, Mary said, had once belonged to Gillespie House but had all been sold off long since.

The other drive, along which Nat had seen the police coming for him, joined ours at a spread of gravel in front of the house. The house itself was far from a 'stately home', but big enough that I'd have hated to have to keep it clean or pay the heating bills. It was typical of the area, more than a hundred years old but well looked after, although at a closer look I saw that the signs of loving maintenance over many years had given way to a more slapdash approach, coping with the worst and giving the rest a lick and a promise, so to speak. There were the signs that a caring but unskilled hand had used a paintbrush on the twelve-paned windows, painstakingly removing most of the dribbles from the glass but not even trying to clean the drips off the stone sills. And if I'd been the owner I'd have had most of the ivy and Virginia creeper off it.

But although I'm not going to pretend that I know about styles and proportions (I leave that sort of thing to Keith and his friends) I'll just say that it looked glad to be there and a happy house to live in.

For once my uncle has hit the nail on the head.

131

*When I came to visit Gillespie House I thought that
it was quite beautiful, but I couldn't have said why.
If I could have persuaded Dad to act as my guarantor
I would have made an offer on the spot.*

Mary ignored the old-fashioned bell-pull and
pressed a modern illuminated button. I thought that
I heard a bell ring in the distance but nobody came.

'She's out,' Keith said – with relief, I thought. 'We
should have phoned first.'

Mary frowned. 'I thought the idea was to drop in
very casually,' she said. 'Anyway, Mrs Connerty's
hardly ever out, and then it's usually a Thursday
when a neighbour gives her a lift to St Boswell for
her shopping. She'll likely be in the garden. Come
on.'

She set off round the house, following another bit
of driveway which led to some outbuildings and then
to what was evidently a farm track heading away up
a hill crowned by a gorse-covered hump. The house
was set in several acres of garden, edged with hedges
and a screen of mature birch. The garden had once
been beautiful. There were still splashes of colour
from old plantings of spring bulbs and early flower-
ing shrubs. But vegetables had been planted
between the shrubs, the lawns were overgrown and
the roses long overdue for pruning and the beds had
been given the hasty pretence of weeding that looks
good for a day or two but in reality only divides the
roots of the weeds and buries their seeds, ensuring
more vigorous growth for later.

From somewhere beyond a roughly trimmed yew
hedge we could hear an educated lady's voice. And
I don't mean just the accent although she did sound

just like Lady Hay. It's a funny thing about the English language; so many other languages have been brought into it that there's a dozen different words for almost anything and yet only one of each counts as a proper swear-word. As a result, when you're really put out and need a safety valve to release the pressure, you can only produce a truly satisfying mouthful by stringing the few available words together in new and imaginative ways, which can be done best by somebody with an education to call on and a fund of quotations to use as a framework.

Mary put a stop to a highly educated piece of abuse by cooeeing hastily and leading us through an archway in the nearest hedge. Squatting beside a large motor-mower was the lady concerned. She looked tired. She was sucking a bleeding knuckle, there were streaks of oil on her hands and face, her hair was all kerfuffled and she was wearing a tattered suit of overalls which were much too large for her so that she had had to roll up the sleeves and legs. And yet, as she straightened up, none of that mattered. I had never really met her, just seen her in the distance and that not for a number of years, not since she had left Newton Lauder. She must be in her forties by now and there were signs of it in the lines around her mouth and on her neck, but she had kept her figure and her bones were good so that, even without make-up, she remained a real beauty. Mary, who was close to my ideal of a woman, faded by comparison. Not that I thought any the less of Mary, you understand – I take her for what she is, a woman at my level in the world, and as such she's as fine looking as any, while Mrs Connerty

133

was unreal, as remote as a film star, to be admired but never touched.

Mary introduced me as her fiancé. Mrs Connerty smiled and pulled a cloth from a pocket in her overalls to wipe her hand before shaking mine. Her hand was slender but it felt as strong and as rough as a man's. 'I wish you both very happy,' she said. 'If I have a regret it's that this means I've little chance of getting Mary back to work here ... even if I do get my finances in order.'

Before anyone could take advantage of the opening, she shook hands with Keith very formally but I could see tiny signals of recognition and remembering passing between them. She turned quickly to Ian. Keith introduced him as 'My son-in-law, Ian,' but there was nothing wrong with either Mrs Connerty's memory or her manners. 'The policeman,' she said. 'How nice to meet you, off duty. You must all come in. I'll put the kettle on.' She gave the mower a look of intense dislike. 'I think this thing passed away, regretted by none. Leave it to rot. I'll get the farmer to come in and cut the grass with his tractor. He can tow that thing away at the same time. He owes me a favour.'

There was a time when Keith would have jumped through hoops for the chance to go indoors with the gorgeous and popular Miss Mathieson, as she was then. Now, he froze like a rabbit. I still think that it was temptation he was afraid of rather than the woman herself, but I swear that I saw his hair stand up. 'We'll take a look at it for you,' he said.

'Would you? Well, if you think resuscitation would work my prayers will be with you.'

We three men clustered round the patient and let Mary go in with our hostess for a bout of girl-talk.

134

I cleaned up the electrics while Keith went back to his car for his can of spare petrol and some tools. He washed the air filter and then set about adjusting the blades. Ian gave the moving parts some long overdue lubrication.

At first pull, the four-stroke motor began to purr. It sounded slightly rough but very grateful for the attention. Keith let the clutch in and guided the mower around what seemed to have been the perimeter of the lawn although in places it was difficult to make out where lawn ended and beds began. Ian and I gathered up the tools and materials.

'Shouldn't you be inside, quizzing Mrs Connerty?' I asked. 'I thought that that was what we came for.'

'They'll be too busy picking you to pieces to bother with anybody else for at least another half-hour,' Ian said. Since his own wedding, he had learned a lot. 'Anyway, Mary knows what to ask about if they should start to reminisce.'

Keith came round again. The mower was struggling. The grass was already too long to be easily cut. It needed a scything first but there was no time for that.

At the far side of the lawn, the machine's note rose for a second. Keith slipped it out of gear and stopped for a look. We joined him. The mower had just passed over a stone slab which was sunk flush with the ground. It was largely covered with moss but when Keith scraped this away with the edge of his sole some curved lines appeared and became a rough outline drawing of what seemed to be two fat babies, or possibly Buddhas.

I shivered in spite of myself. 'It looks like a gravestone,' I suggested.

'I hope they don't have a tradition of burying

babies in the garden.' Ian sounded more like a policeman than ever.

Keith laughed. 'So do I,' he said. 'But I suggest that you think about the signs of the zodiac and in particular the Heavenly Twins. I think that this is where Nat's favourite dog lies buried.'

'Thank God for that!' Ian said. I took several deep breaths. Ian's words had started a chain of thought which I was glad not to follow through.

'And now,' said Keith, 'one of you can take over while I stow my things away in the car.'

'I'll do it. You go and get your tea,' I told Ian.

I made a few small adjustments and started up again. It was very pleasant, steering the now smoothly running mower round and round in the spring sunshine. I found the compost heap, emptied the sweet-smelling mowings and went on until one lawn at least was part-way back to respectability. Another cut with the blades lowered would see it fit for a game of bowls, almost. The shadows had grown longer and when I stopped the little engine the crows were processing overhead on their way home.

There was an outhouse door standing open, so I guessed that that was where the mower spent its days on standby. Another shed, open-fronted, held logs and an evil-looking old handsaw. I found my way through the back door into a kitchen. There was no hot water in the tap so I heated a kettle to wash, just as I could see that the others had done before me.

I followed the distant sound of voices but on the way I kept my eyes open. I saw places where repair had been attempted by a loving but amateur hand

and others where work and tools had been abandoned for the moment in favour of some more urgent task. The rooms were large and lofty but most were now semi-derelict, stripped of anything sellable and protected only from the worst ravages of damp and fungus. The overall picture was of a battle made hopeless by a total lack of money.

The voices led me up a broad, curving stair to the upper floor. A narrower stair went on up to the attics, but I found the company in a sitting-room, small by the standards of that house but huge compared to mine, above the front door. It was the only room which I had seen fully furnished. The others were taking tea and home-made scones from fine but imperfectly matched china. A small log fire had been laid but not lit and the room was cool.

The chairs were fancy but comfortable and sturdier than they looked. I took the one that seemed to have been reserved for me and Mrs Connerty poured me some tea. 'I looked out once or twice,' she said, 'but you seemed to be quite happy and I certainly wasn't going to put you off from cutting my grass. I'm grateful.'

'My pleasure,' I said.

Keith put down his cup on a little rosewood table. 'What you need,' he told Mrs Connerty, 'is a few sheep. If I lent you a length of electric fence, which you could move from time to time, your friend the farmer would probably be delighted to pasture half a dozen ewes with their lambs here all summer. He'd probably let you have a lamb, ready for the freezer, to pay for the extra grazing.'

I looked at Keith sharply. The only electric fence he could put his hands on, as far as I knew, would mostly be made up of the anti-fox electric wires that we ran round the release pens on our shoot.

'And that means that I'd never have to wrestle with that monster again? Keith, you'd be my saviour!'

For once in his life my articulate brother-in-law seemed to have lost his tongue.

I saw Ian give Mary a tiny nod as a signal. 'You must find it all a bit much for you,' Mary said, 'trying to keep this place up all by yourself.'

Mrs Connerty made a little gesture, half humorous and half despairing. 'Sometimes I think it's altogether too much for me,' she said, 'but at least I'll go down fighting. I know – and you know too, Mary – that I love the place too much to let it go to rack and ruin. And, of course, it's all I've got left of my husband.' She grinned suddenly with a wry sort of amusement. 'I dare say that you wouldn't have trusted Nat as far as you could spit, and you'd have been right. Starting from nothing, he needed to show the world and himself that he could put it over on any of them. And he was doing it all for me even if I'd have been happy to settle for less, honestly won.' She sighed. 'That's just the way he was. But with me he was different. I could have trusted him to the ends of the earth and known that he wouldn't let me down. So I hang on, hoping against all reason that something will happen to pluck me out of my difficulties. Unfortunately I'm a little bit long in the tooth to expect a Prince Charming. Hope, yes. Expect, no.'

There was a moment's hiccup in the conversation as we each searched for a noncommittal answer. It was Keith who decided to stay with the strictly practical. 'Couldn't you let the place?' he asked. 'Move

138

to somewhere smaller and easier to manage while some big firm keeps the place in repair for you and pays you a rent to live on?'

'I thought of that,' Mrs Connerty said. 'But, just in case I ever have tuppence to rub together again, I'd want to be able to get them out quickly, but anybody prepared to take over a place this size wants a lease of at least twenty years.'

Ian was frowning at Keith. Problem solving was not the turn he wanted the conversation to take. I decided to help out. 'Nat was never daft, no matter what he sometimes pretended,' I said. 'Surely some of his money must have survived, somewhere?'

'You would think so,' said Mrs Connerty. She looked and sounded a wee bit bored and I supposed that a good many people must have chatted her up in the hope of clues to Nat's vanished hoard. 'I'll tell you something that I've only told the police. You don't mind?' she added to Ian.

'Not in the least.' It was my guess that Ian hadn't the faintest idea what was coming.

'I never spied on Nat. I knew that he'd tell me what I needed to know. And so he would have done if he'd had time. But after he was killed, every bank account of every individual business in the group turned up empty or overdrawn. I knew that he was collecting cash, because several times I saw him take fat wads out of his briefcase. American dollars mostly, so maybe that's where he was planning to take us.'

'More likely it was because dollars pass anywhere,' Keith said. 'And the Americans print larger denominations than we do, so a big sum would go into a smaller package.'

She nodded. 'Could be. On top of all that money

out of the businesses, I'm told that there should have been a whole lot more from his cash dealings. I know that he owned a metal box, rather like a suitcase. There was no trace of it in the car and it certainly wasn't in the house. The police had a damn good look for it and so did I.'

Ian caught me looking at him out of the corner of my eye. 'Don't even dream that one of the police might have found it, Ronnie,' he said. 'If that had happened, some kind of whisper would have reached me by now.'

'Perhaps he was driving towards where he'd hidden it when he . . . crashed,' Mrs Connerty said. 'Poor Nat!' She suppressed another sigh and then looked at Ian. 'Was that what you wanted to ask me?' There was a trace of a smile. I was reminded again of what a beauty she had been when we were young.

Ian was looking abashed. 'We called in because Mary wanted to tell you her news,' he said. 'But, since we're here . . . would you mind if I asked you something?'

'Not a lot. Every other bugger's taken a turn. At least, as a policeman, you have some standing.'

Ian nodded. I think that he had to make an effort not to look shocked. 'The money is almost a side issue,' he said. 'Very important to those it properly belongs to and, of course, it's one of the concerns of the police to get it back for them. Your husband's death can be explained. I'm much more concerned about the other man who died.'

For the first time, she showed real surprise. 'Dan Graham? But the sheriff brought it in as a suicide. God knows he stood to lose enough money in Nat's crash. Nat certainly couldn't have killed him.'

'I've been reading up the case,' Ian said. 'The police files and the transcript of the inquiry before the sheriff. There are certain discrepancies. They could be inadvertent – the outcome of sloppily prepared evidence. I rather think that the procurator fiscal wanted to put it away tidily and the sheriff helped by listening to his widow's evidence and jumping to a conclusion.'

Mrs Connerty raised one eyebrow. 'The money was mostly Mrs Graham's rather than his – she'd brought money into the marriage and set him up in his business in agricultural chemicals and she's kept it up since he died. But she didn't seem too concerned about the money. Perhaps there was more where it came from.

'He was the one who got uptight about the money. She had quite a different bee in her bonnet. She was convinced that he was having an affair with me. She was up here that morning, carrying on like a fishwife. As if I'd have had him even if he'd come with a certificate of studworthiness and a pound of fish! He was rather older than the hills and I don't want to speak ill of the dead but, really, he did look like something that an angler would give to the cat.'

'I never knew that she was here that morning,' Mary said. 'I didn't hear a car.'

'Well, you wouldn't,' Mrs Connerty said. 'You were tucked away in the kitchen. And Dougie had been sleeping late after his trip and then helped me in the garden. That's how she came to walk in on us. They were both here that morning. Not together, I think. And I don't think that either of them brought a car to the house. Naturally. We wouldn't

141

have let either of them inside if we'd known they were there, those were Nat's orders. They lived – she still lives – within walking distance if you don't mind a good leg-stretch, but they could leave a car at the old quarry and walk over the hill if they wanted to.'

She stopped, as though that topic was exhausted. Ian said, 'Please tell me about that day.'

She looked at him for a few seconds before she nodded. 'Nat went out after breakfast. We'd been plagued with carrion crows, so he took a gun out to see if he could catch one or two of them on the hop. He knew by then that he was going to have to ... emigrate, but it was still habit with him to try and keep the crows down. He'd sold the land off much earlier to finance some deal or other, but he retained the sporting rights and he had a small shoot, just for himself and a few friends or business contacts. You were invited once, I remember,' she added to Keith. 'The crows were sudden death to eggs or fledgelings.

'Dan Graham must have seen him from the hill because he came up with him and started a long argument. Nat told me about it later. Mr Graham wanted his money back. I gather that he called Nat a whole lot of names and said that he'd been swindled and Nat said that if he had a little patience he'd get his money back along with his share of the profits.' Mrs Connerty paused and had the grace to blush. 'I'm afraid that Nat wasn't always very truthful.

'After about half an hour, Nat lost his patience, or so he told me later. He told Dan Graham to get off his property and when the man wouldn't go and went on slanging him – and, incidentally, warning

142

the crows off – Nat explained, quite politely, that there was going to be a very sad accident with a shotgun in about half a minute but that it would turn out to be the dead man's own fault for suddenly stepping in front of the man with the gun. Mr Graham said that he was going to tell the police that he'd been threatened and Nat asked whether he was really trying to make sure that Nat shot him dead there and then. He changed his tune after that and walked back towards the quarry through the garden and Nat followed along for most of the way just to make sure that he went.

'I only witnessed the absolute tail end of their confrontation for myself while I was pottering in the garden. They stopped near by. I think that they were both too het up to notice me, but Dan Graham was beginning to cool off and being more conciliatory by then. He went so far as to apologize, saying that he still wanted to get his money out but that he'd had no right to lose his rag over it. He even popped a cigar into Nat's top pocket – enjoyment of a good cigar was about the only thing they had in common – and said, "No hard feelings, then?" As far as I can remember, Nat didn't answer him.'

'You never told the police any of this,' Ian said – rather gently, I thought.

'If you read over the transcripts, you'll find that I didn't tell any lies. I answered the questions exactly as they were asked and nobody thought to ask me whether either of the Grahams had come to this house earlier that day. It didn't seem relevant – it still doesn't. After all, it only goes to support the sheriff's verdict. And also it didn't exactly show any of us in a very good light.'

'I see,' said Ian. 'And what about Mrs Graham?'

143

'She was kind of spooky,' Mrs Connerty admitted with an uneasy laugh. 'I'd been in and out of the garden-room French windows, cutting some flowers and doing some odd jobs in the garden, because although Nat had told me by then that he was going to have to go abroad I'd rather more than half a mind to stay here and stick it out. If it had come to the point, I don't know which I'd have chosen – my house or my husband. You see,' she said simply, 'I loved them both. I hadn't been a party to any of Nat's little games and I didn't fancy trying to make new friends, find my way around and probably learn a new language in some foreign hellhole. Nat had made it clear that he wanted to head for the sunshine, but heat brings me out in a rash. Nat understood, though I think he was sure that I'd get fed up after a few months without him and come rushing to his side.' She showed us her smile again. 'Under it all, he was a romantic at heart. But of course he had said that if I wanted to stay here he could leave me provided for. I didn't expect to be left damn near penniless. Not Nat's fault,' she added quickly. 'He didn't expect it to work out this way.'

'Mrs Graham,' Ian said patiently.

She nodded an apology. 'I've strayed, haven't I? Perverse and foolish, just like in the hymn, that's me.' The quotation came easily off her tongue. 'When I came in for the umpteenth time, I had a vase of flowers for this room so I came through into the hall. And I met Mrs Graham there, looking even more of a sight than usual in slacks that showed her bum to worst advantage. She'd had the gall to walk in, knowing damn well we'd have left her on the doorstep.'

144

'Wasn't the door locked?' Ian asked. He sounded shocked, as a good policeman should.

'Who locks doors in the country? She didn't say anything about money, just got stuck into me right away for trying to take her husband away from her, of all the idiotic things!

'I wasn't going to lower myself to her level. I just told her that if I had wanted her husband I could have taken him away without even trying, but that as it was I wouldn't have had him if you'd paid me.' (*An exaggeration?*) 'I may also have mentioned that if, for some strange reason, she really wanted to hang onto that husband of hers, she'd better lay off the jealousy kick and the starchy foods.' Mrs Connerty put a hand to her mouth. 'In view of what happened I wish I could take the last bit back, but at least after that she went almost quietly.'

Keith had been listening intently but in silence. 'How long could she have been in the house?' he asked suddenly.

'Ages, I suppose. The main part of the house had been empty, apart from Mary in the kitchen and me in and out of the garden-room. Why?'

'Think about it,' Keith said. 'Doesn't it seem rather odd that they should each have arrived at around the same time, to badger the two of you on two different subjects?'

Mrs Connerty looked thoughtful. 'You always did peer that little bit deeper,' she said. 'It comes of being a twisted sort of character yourself. You and Nat would have made a fine pair of bookends – just the same but opposite ways round. Yes, now that you mention it, it seems a bit of a coincidence and rather out of key. What are you suggesting?'

145

'Could they have known that Nat was stockpiling cash?'

'Almost certainly. They were pally with Julian Wincherly, Nat's Financial Director. It was on his introduction that they'd invested with Nat.'

'Was your meeting with her before or after Nat's parting from her husband?'

'After. Only a few minutes, though. Dan Graham went off towards the hill. Nat went back to the crows. I took my flowers indoors and there she was. Nat gave up and came indoors a few minutes after I'd got rid of her. Why?'

Keith shrugged off the question. 'There you are, then. They wanted their money out before the inevitable crash. They knew that Nat was turning everything into portable cash, so it must have been obvious that he was planning to run for it. They probably kept watch from the hill. When Nat went out and they could see you in the garden, he went to keep Nat busy while she searched the house.'

'A tall order for one woman, a house search,' Ian commented. 'I'd have brought ten officers with me for a place this size.'

'She was looking for a large slab of banknotes in something like a suitcase,' Keith said, 'not a fingerprint. They knew that Nat couldn't make a fuss with the police if he found most but not all of the money had vanished. You must have caught her on her way out. She didn't want to mention money for fear of setting the bells ringing so she fell back on the only other story she could think up in a hurry. Does that make more sense?'

'It certainly does. Do you think—?'

'I shouldn't think so. Not unless she had a metal suitcase hidden about her person.'

146

'With her figure,' Mrs Connerty said thoughtfully, 'you could hardly tell. She could have lowered the case out of a window, I suppose. But I don't believe she'd scored. What she said was vicious rather than triumphant. And he wouldn't have had good reason to jump if she'd been able to put her hands on the money.'

'Whatever else happened,' Ian said, 'I'm fairly sure of one thing. He didn't jump.'

Nobody asked him why he was so sure. I think that we had each begun to have doubts about the sheriff's verdict.

SEVEN

Molly had been drumming it into me that if I did not want Mary to go the way of the others I should try to remember to be the perfect little gentleman as our mother had tried to teach us. So I held the door for her and let Keith and Ian go ahead of me. Before I could follow, Mrs Connerty, who had hung back, took my sleeve. 'You're in touch with Dougie, aren't you?' she asked softly.

'How did you know?' I asked.

She smelled like a whole garden of flowers and for once I didn't mind. She was no chicken but she had the most beautiful eyes I've ever seen except in a red deer hind, and her mouth was the kind that men would die to kiss.

'Never mind how I knew.'

'He phoned you?' As I spoke, I guessed that Dougie had been making use of the phone kiosk in the Square during the hours of darkness. But then I remembered that, about a fortnight earlier, I'd heard some gype complaining that his car had been entered when he parked it in the Square overnight and the thief had pinched the mobile phone which he should have had more sense than to leave in the car and had made calls on it before the silly gowk got around to having the service cut off. The police would long since have given up the demanding business of phone tapping and if they ever got around to wondering why the gype's phone bill showed a call to the lady, she could say that the call had been from a pervert trying to chat her up and that she'd kept him talking in the hope of finding out who he was.

She nodded reluctantly. 'The week before last. The police had opened his safe at the time of the bust up and impounded everything in it. I dare say he could make them give him his money if he came forward, but it could be years before he was free to spend it. He wouldn't get the passports anyway; they'd been stolen out of cars and the photographs fudged. Can you get this to him? He dropped it once when he was using my car and I found it under the seat. I meant to give it back to him but the bust-up came before I remembered to do it. The police never found it and I'd forgotten all about it until his phone call. He wants it.'

She gave me a sealed envelope. I took it reluctantly as it meant the end of our intimate talk. The hard rectangle inside was about the size and shape of a passport.

'I'll see that he gets it,' I said.

As we got into the car, I looked up. Mrs Connerty was standing in the sitting-room window and when she saw me looking she waved. We sat quietly for a moment, each of us thinking.

'It's a shame,' I said. 'A nice-like wifie like that struggling to keep her house together on her own, and with all that garden to see to. She'll be needing the vegetables to keep her body and soul together, if she spends what money she can get on the house.'

'Yes,' said the others.

'Maybe,' I said, 'I should go over and dig the beds for her, an evening or two.'

'No,' said the others in unison, so sharply that I jumped. 'Not unless I'm with you,' Mary said firmly. 'She's a real lady, but she only knows one way to thank a gentleman for his help.'

'She'd suck you dry and blow you out in little bubbles,' Keith added as a sort of explanation. 'Shall we just take a look at where it happened?'

'Since we're here,' Ian agreed.

Keith drove past the outbuildings, bypassed the garden and followed the farm track up the easy slope. 'Why are you so interested in an old death that the sheriff wrote off as a suicide?' he asked Ian.

'I have never been happy with the sheriff's decision. There was just too much coincidence. And then there was something that was glossed over at the inquiry. There were marks on the ground at the lip of the quarry. From the photographs on file they look to me like the marks of a struggle, but the procurator fiscal preferred to think that they were the marks of a man who made little runs at the brink but lost his nerve each time and pulled up. Except the last time, of course. The sheriff must have agreed with him.'

'Uh-huh. Here we are,' Keith said.

We had been bumping gently up the farm track, but the track turned aside to follow a contour round the large hump that crowned the hill. The quarry had been excavated into the side of the hump so that its floor was level with the track. Keith pulled over and parked on the level floor of the quarry and he and Ian got out.

'I remember this place,' Keith said. 'Nat placed three or four guns in the quarry – that was as many as he ever invited – and the old keeper with a few mates would drive the pheasants off the top. And, believe me, they were real screamers, high and fast and curling. Quality beats quantity any day.'

'I believe you,' I said through the open door. The rock wall must have been forty yards high, just about one permissible gunshot.

'You can go out to play,' Mary told me. 'I'll be quite happy to sit here and look at the view.'

I had dug my own garden that morning and mown Mrs Connerty's biggest lawn in the afternoon, and truth to tell I'm not quite as young as I was. My legs wanted to stay where they were but, if I had said as much, Keith would have crowed over me for ever. I got out and joined the others. When I looked round I could see a cottage beside the public road on a facing slope. It had been hidden from me by the hedge bordering the farm track while I was seated in the car. Dusk was creeping in and I saw a light come on. Keith was looking in the same direction. 'I think that that's where old McKee, the keeper, used to live,' he said.

'I think he still does,' said Ian. 'He was interviewed but he hadn't seen anything useful. He'd attended to the feeding and hardly even glanced this way again. And, of course, cars parked here would be out of his sight from there.'

'He could have seen them turning off the road,' Keith said.

'He could but he didn't.' Ian looked as though he'd just bitten into a bad apple. 'Of course not. Typical of that case. Anybody who was in the right place at the right time had his eyes shut. No wonder

151

if justice miscarried. It's enough to give anyone an abortion.'

'If you ask me,' Keith said, 'which you didn't, I'd say that you're baying for the moon, thinking to upset the sheriff's verdict after – what is it? – two years?'

Ian nodded sadly. 'Two years almost to the day. And my superiors – long may they remain far away in Auld Reekie – would blow their collective tops if I expended a lot of time and came up with anything less than a rock-solid proof. All the same, the most intractable cases are often the ones in which, suddenly, the vital witness appears out of nowhere or the crucial piece of evidence is handed in. Sometimes it turns out to have been staring everyone in the face all along.'

'If I were you, I wouldn't hold my breath,' Keith said.

'Believe me, I'm not. But I'll soldier on for a little bit longer. Let's take a look up top.'

'If you think you'll learn anything,' Keith said.

'If I don't look, I won't know.'

I was on the point of getting back into the car in the hope of a cuddle with Mary during their absence when Keith called to me to follow along.

'There'll be nothing there after all this time,' I said.

'There might; and you're the tracker,' was all the answer I got. Sometimes it doesn't pay to be good at something.

We set off up the slope beside the quarry's flank, followed a sheep track through some gorse bushes and came out near the crest of the hill. A wide expanse of gorse and scattered trees crowned the hill, but a broad ride had been cut through the middle, opening out on the very lip of the quarry into what was almost a terrace where the birds could dry off and take the sun. The ride was beginning to choke now with fresh growth but I could see that it had at one time been well strawed. Feeding the birds in straw keeps them too busy to get into mischief or to wander, but of course it has to be done oftener than with feed-hoppers. (*In this context, birds means pheasants.*) Some low corrugated metal shelters had fallen into disrepair. Somewhere among the gorse I heard a cock pheasant chortle, so there were at least a few survivors or descendants of Nat Connerty's releases.

Grass and weeds had grown up through any traces which might otherwise have remained. In places, grain which had been scattered in the straw had germinated, creating an unlikely fuzz through the weeds. There was no sign of human presence. Presumably if the local poacher still made occasional visits he was too careful to drop handkerchieves and cigarette ends about the place.

'We're not going to learn anything here,' Ian said disgustedly. 'Let's go.'

There was something nagging at me but I hesitated before speaking out and the moment passed. I followed the other two down the hill.

When the car had moved off, Ian said, 'I suppose that you're all busting to get home for tea?' in a questioning sort of voice. I looked at the dashboard clock. That sort of question in that sort of tone usually precedes a suggestion that we visit the nearest pub, which would just have opened its doors, so I said that there was no hurry at all.

153

'I'm still enjoying my day out,' Mary said.

'Oh, well,' Keith said. 'What did you have in mind?'

'I'd like to pay a call on old Ken McKee at the cottage there.'

'I suppose you'll girn all the way home if we don't,' Keith said. But something told me that he was getting interested. There's a change in his voice when he's getting his teeth into a problem. Perhaps his mouth's full of it.

He turned at the mouth of the farm track and soon pulled onto the verge outside the cottage. At the sound of the car the door opened, spilling light into the gathering dusk, and a man looked out and then approached down the path. He must have been in his sixties and against the light he looked frail, but later I saw that although he was thin he was wiry and muscular. Keith got out of the car but held the door open so that the interior light stayed on. 'Visitors, Mr McKee,' he said. 'Remember me?'

'Aye, I mind you fine. You've sold me a bonny puckle o' cartridges afore now.' Ken McKee stooped and looked into the car. His face creased into a huge smile, showing unnatural teeth. 'Bless us, it's Mary Millburn came back to see us. Mary Jablinska, I should say. And young Ron Fiddler. You were at school wi' my son Jock. I mind that you and this lassie were aye a pair.'

'We've just got engaged,' Mary said.

'About twenty years late, but better late than never. Come awa' intil the house for a dram.'

I think that Keith was about to refuse the invitation, but I was dying for a dram after all my work and Ian wanted the excuse to ask some questions

154

so we both got out. I helped Mary up. Keith sighed. 'And this is my son-in-law, Ian Fellowes,' he said.

'The policeman,' Ken said, nodding. It's easy to forget how gossip travels in the countryside. 'Come on in. My brother Gus is here, back from Canada. You'll remember him?'

We trooped inside, past suitcases in the hall, and found chairs in the cramped but cheerful sitting-room. The room was still warm though the fire had been allowed to die. A mongrel dog that looked to be half collie and about a quarter Labrador was lying on the hearth.

I remembered Jock's Uncle Angus as an upstanding man who had taken prizes at the Highland Games. One hardly notices the ageing process in the folk one sees every day because it is so gradual but, not having seen Angus McKee for a matter of thirty years and since a time when he would have looked larger because I was smaller, I was startled to see how much he had shrunk from what I remembered. But when I looked from him to his brother I saw that they were as like as two eggs in a nest, except that Ken would have vanished in a crowd of church-goers while Gus wore a checked suit and a tie that would have shone in the dark. It was also noticeable that Gus's teeth had come from a more expensive source and, although he had kept the accent of his youth, his turns of phrase were now mostly Canadian.

There were glasses on the table beside a half-empty bottle of whisky and one still unopened. Ken pressed each of us to take a dram. Keith took one look at the brand and was happy to plead that he could take the merest taste because he was driving.

155

In his old age, Keith is becoming a whisky snob.

Gus's memory was still as perfect as his brother's. Only Mary and Ian had to be introduced to him; he remembered Keith and myself from our boyhood and was ready to produce a fund of scurrilous stories that we had to choke off rather hastily for fear that they might have found their way back to Molly. But manners required that we update him briefly on our life histories since those days and to listen to the story of how he had emigrated to join a cousin in Canada and, rather than become a farmer himself, had made an adequate living as a merchant in grain and seeds. 'I never got what you'd call rich,' he said, 'but I retired when I reckoned I could be comfortable. Put my little pile into offshore capital bonds in the Isle of Man. They cough up at this time of year and I come over to collect my profit and plough the rest back in.' He spent a few minutes explaining some dodge that sounded highly illegal to me but saved him a fortune in tax. Unfortunately it passed over my head.

'Did you say that you always come here at this time of year?' Ian asked sharply.

'That's right. I'll fly out from Renfrew in the morning.'

'If you wait a wee while you'll meet Jock again,' said Ken. 'He aye drives us through to Glasgow, bides a couple of days and brings me back again. We'll party half the night away with my sister's family. Angus can sleep it off on the plane and I'll do the rounds of my Glasgow relatives.'

'You'll remember Bessie?' Ken added to Keith. If the two had been sitting closer I think that a nudge would have followed.

Ian refused to let Keith be diverted. 'But you visited here two years ago?' he asked.

'I surely did.'

'You know that there was a fatality at the quarry?' Gus nodded. 'Was that while you were here?'

'Well now,' Gus said slowly. 'That's kind of a moot point. I knew nothing about it except for a passing mention in Ken's letters – we're not much for letter-writing, either of us. But he told me some more when I came visiting a year back. He told me that Nat Connerty had killed himself in a smash about the time that we were leaving for Glasgow – in fact, we'd been passed by the ambulance and a fire appliance without knowing what it was about or where they were heading. I can't say as I was sur-prised to hear about Nat, I remember him as a boy and he was always a wild one. As I understand it, the other man was found about the time I was taking off for home. But as to whether I was still here when he fell, that's another matter.'

'Well, were you?' Ian asked patiently.

'You tell me what time he fell and I'll answer the question.'

'We don't know what time he fell,' Ian admitted. I noticed that each had decided to refer to falling rather than jumping. Suicide is a sensitive topic, to be avoided whenever possible. He rounded on Ken. 'You never said anything about your brother being here at the time.'

'At what time?' Ken asked blandly. 'I answered whatever I was asked. I still don't know if he was here when the mannie jumped.'

There were too many possible answers to that. Ian thought it over and decided not to bother. 'It

157

seems possible that the fall may not have been due to suicide. You do remember that afternoon?' he asked Angus.

'I surely do.'

'Did you see anything at all happening near the quarry?'

Angus nodded several times, thoughtfully. 'I guess I did. Most years on my last day here, just like today, Ken and I have a shot or three of whisky while we wait for Jock to come for us. That's how it was last year. But that day, two years back, Ken hadn't finished packing his case.'

'I'd been busy,' Ken said. 'After lunch, I went up to the hill above the quarry to scatter some feed in the strawed ride for the pheasants that had been left on the ground, enough to see them through until I got back. Spring's as bad as winter for the birds to go short and wander off. It seems like a time of plenty but in fact you don't get seeds or insects until later than you'd think.'

I was going to ask whether it was wheat that he was scattering but Keith was impatient. 'We do know that,' he said.

'Aye. Well, when I got up there, a fox had been among them. I could see where he'd crept under cover of a bush and pounced on a hen. The birds would be nesting soon and a fox could have a high old time among them. So I came back down for Jacko' – the mongrel opened one eye and gave a single thump of his tail – 'and my gun and a pocketful of snares. I wasnae wanting to use the snares – it'd mean asking Mr Connerty to visit them while I was awa', but he was aye busy and more so than usual just then. I kenned he'd want me to manage for mysel'.'

'Could Bruce, his brother, not have done it for you?' Ian asked.

Ken shook his head emphatically. 'Bruce Connerty took no interest in the shoot. I doubt if he'd held a gun or climbed the hill in his life, let alone set a snare. So I took Jacko to where the bird had been killed. He's a clever old devil when it comes to tracking and he's no lover of foxes. And we went gey softly through the cover, just following Jacko's nose, and' – his voice rose with remembered triumph – 'dashed if we didn't come up on the fox, sound asleep in the sunshine between a wall and some gorse.' Ken mimed pulling a trigger. 'That was the end of Mr Fox. And it was the last bit of keepering I got to do. When I came back from Glasgow I heard that Mr Connerty was dead and I was out of a job. It's not good enough sporting land to attract a shooting syndicate. Mrs Connerty lets the sporting rights to a couple of young fellows from Newton Lauder but they do for themselves what little keepering gets done.'

Gus had waited indulgently while the other rambled on. Now he picked up where his brother had left off. 'I was on my own in here for much of the afternoon. When Ken came down off the hill he was dusty and sweaty and in no state to go visiting in Glasgow and he still had his packing to attend to. Away he went to shower and pack, and I had nothing much to do except to look out of the window and see if Jock was coming yet. It wouldn't have been mannerly to start the drinking on my own.'

'At last we're coming to it,' Ian said. 'What did you see?'

'I saw two people. One at a time. I don't know if

159

this is what you want but it's all that I saw. First I heard a car and I saw a man climb up from the quarry. He went up slowly like an old man, and I could see that he was mostly bald and what hair he had was grey-brown.'

'That,' said Ian, 'sounds very much like Mr Graham, the man who died. How did he look? Happy? Or fed up to the back teeth?'

'He looked kind of pleased with himself. Only minutes later I heard another car and somebody else climbed the hill, but not so slowly. And, just after that, Ken came back, all clean and tidy and with his bag packed, and we opened the bottle and Jock rolled up not long after.'

Ian closed his eyes in exasperation for a moment. 'The second person. It was a man, not a woman?'

'I'd say so. The face could've been either but it didn't seem to me to be wide enough across the butt for a woman. And the shoulders were too wide.'

'Can you describe him?' he asked.

'I don't know as I can, no more'n I have already.'

'I realize that it was two years ago . . .'

'It ain't that,' Angus said. 'If it was yesterday, I still couldn't tell you any more. I saw him pretty good and I remember him well, for all the good that'll do you. There was nothing near him to tell me if he was large or small. He was neither fat nor thin. His clothes were plain and ordinary and he wore one of those flat caps that most folks wear around these parts. His hair seemed short and I couldn't make a guess at what colour it was. The only part of him that I'd know again was his face. And how do you describe a face when there's nothing special about it? I remember it. I got a good

160

memory for faces and, besides, it put me in mind of one of my neighbours back home. I'd know it again. But I can't describe it.'

That seemed reasonable to me. If a face has no whiskers and is too far off for you to see the colour of its eyes and eyebrows, what can you say about it? Somebody said once that a millimetre is big if it's on the end of a woman's nose, or something of the sort. That millimetre may make all the difference to the woman's appearance, but how do you describe that difference?

'It would surely be one of only three or four men,' Ian said. 'If you got a good look at them, could you pick him out for me? Or make a Photofit of him?'

Angus flashed a gold wristwatch. 'I guess I could. But it'd have to be in the next hour or so.'

Ian's sandy hair seemed to bristle. 'Surely in the interests of justice—'

'My ticket,' Angus said firmly, 'is Apex. If I don't make the plane I pay over again and it costs me more. You planning to reimburse me?'

I saw Ian cringe. 'Well, no,' he said.

'There you are, then. What's more, our kinfolk in Glasgow are expecting us. What's more still, my son will be on the road by now in his camper, heading to pick me up from the airport, and I've no way of reaching him. Nope, you want to keep me back you better get yourself a court order.'

'And a fat chance I've got of that,' Ian said bitterly. 'A court already decided that David Graham's death was accidental.'

'Then you'd best figure on waiting a year. I guess I've got that much mileage left on my clock.' He paused, waiting for confirmation, but Ian looked

161

uncertain. 'What I could do,' Angus resumed, 'is get together with the cops back home, starting from a photo of my neighbour, and build up an Identikit of the guy. That should tell you who you're after.'

'It's Catch Twenty-two all over again,' Ian said. 'I'll never get authority to bring you back until I've got real evidence and I need to bring you back if I'm to have real evidence. I don't think they'll want to spend public money and go against the sheriff's decision for a sworn statement and an Identikit.'

Silence fell. Ken went round again with the bottle. I waited until my glass was full. 'Look at it this way,' I said to Ian. 'You're probably wondering about Dougie Slattery.'

'I am,' Ian said.

'Well, I don't think the second man could have been Dougie, he'd be too easy to describe and anyway he seems to have been around the house all that day. And even if I told you where he is, which I won't, you couldn't get him together with Angus here in the time. But you've only got to do a deal with him and he'll confirm the identity of the second man.'

'I daren't do it,' Ian said.

'You do have time,' I said, 'to give Angus sight of Bruce Connerty, Nat's brother. And I'm pretty damn sure that Bruce is your man.'

Ian frowned at me and shook his head. 'Mr McKee would have recognized Bruce Connerty,' he said.

'I don't know that I would,' Angus said. 'I don't recall that I ever set eyes on Nat's younger brother.'

'Bruce was Nat's minder and repo man,' I reminded him. 'If Mr Graham meant mischief for

162

Nat, who'd be more likely than Bruce to step in?'

Ian looked at me through slitted eyes. 'You must have more than that,' he said.

'It could have been almost anybody,' I said, 'but, of the ones we know about, the others seem to be accounted for.' I was thinking in particular that the story Harry Fury had told us in the Canal Bar went a long way towards clearing both himself and the financial Mr Wincherly of suspicion. I could see that Mary had followed that line of thought. She was nodding to herself.

Ian would certainly not want me to discuss the identities and the whereabouts of the possible suspects in front of others, but he was on the point of asking me what other reasons I had for blaming Bruce. I could feel it coming and I knew that, however certain was my gut feeling, my reasoning would seem flimsy at best. But there came a rat-tat at the door.

Ken got up. 'That'll be Jock,' he said. 'Sharp as ever.' He went out and returned with a dark young man who towered over his elders. 'We may have a delay here, Jock. Meantime, you could be putting the cases in the car.'

The younger McKee was a man of few if any words. He had acknowledged his uncle's introduction to us with a nod apiece and he accepted the suggestion with another nod.

Ian had had time to sort out his thoughts. 'Let me use your phone,' he said. 'If anything comes of this, I can hardly cram an arrested man into Keith's car along with the four of us. I'll have a couple of officers meet us at Skerriden. And if you're causing me to make an idiot of myself,' he added in my direction, 'the only wedding present you'll get from me will be a summons.'

'For what?' I asked indignantly.

'I don't know yet. But I'll think of something and you won't like it.'

Thinking over my lifestyle of late I decided that he might be spoiled for choice.

While Ian used the phone and Ken McKee prepared the cottage to be unoccupied for a few days, we went out into the night. We got ourselves distributed between the two cars. I noticed that Jacko the mongrel was travelling with Jock and the McKee brothers. Evidently he also was welcome in Glasgow.

'I phoned Deborah,' Ian said as we set off. 'She'll let Molly know that we'll be late.'

Not so very late, I hoped. I was getting hungry.

EIGHT

Keith's car led the way along the quiet night-time roads, followed by the new and shining Toyota driven by Jock with his father and uncle aboard.

'I've given myself a problem,' Ian said as we went, more to himself than to us. 'Assuming that Ronnie hasn't dropped the clanger of the year – which God forbid! – Gus McKee should be able to pick Bruce Connerty as the man who climbed the hill after Daniel Graham. But if Gus is only shown one man, his evidence may be discounted if the matter ever comes to court. But how in hell do I arrange an identity parade with an unwilling suspect, no real authority and a witness who wants to be in Glasgow tonight and Canada tomorrow?'

By then I was on a high, as they say, and buzzing. 'If he picked him out of a crowd, that would be different?'

'Of course,' Ian said impatiently.

'Like in a pub?'

'I think a jury would accept that.'

'Then,' I said, 'I may be the answer to your prayers. I've had a dram or two with Bruce Connerty before now. Not for some years, but he'll remember. I'll go to the door and invite him down to the pub in the village for a drink. I'll say it's my stag night or something.'

'That's good,' Ian said. 'That's very good.' He sounded surprised. Mary squeezed my arm. I glowed. These compliments don't often come my way.

We stopped a hundred yards short of the gate. Keith walked back to explain the programme to the McKee family while I walked to the house and spoke to Doris Lacy. I was back at Keith's car inside a minute. The other car had already vanished.

'He's down at the pub,' I said, getting in.

Keith took off in a hurry. 'Better get down there before they blow it,' he said. 'Just pray that Bruce isn't the only man in the bar.'

Skerriden village was further along the same road, clumped tightly together in a dip. The pub and a small church seemed almost to lean together for mutual support. I saw Jock McKee's car near by with its owner still seated behind the wheel. Keith managed to squeeze his car into a space at the kerb and we trooped inside.

The bar was less than half full but my guess was that there were enough men present to satisfy a jury. Three men, farmers by the look of them, were joking with the formidable looking blonde lady behind the counter. A probably married couple were playing darts, very badly. Bruce Connerty was at a corner table, enjoying a pint in the company of a man in overalls. In the opposite corner, whiskies already in hand, the brothers McKee were seated in a state of barely suppressed excitement. Ian and Mary and I sat down with them while Keith went to the bar for drinks.

166

'Be careful,' Ian said quietly. 'Don't stare or point.'

Angus McKee looked down into his glass. 'We're not as dumb as we look,' he said. 'That's the man in the far corner, with the pale hair and the denim jacket.'

'You're sure?'

'There's no doubt in my mind.'

I saw that one of the men at the bar had been served a hot meat pie and suddenly my mouth was full of saliva. While Ian muttered to Gus McKee, making an arrangement to get a signed statement from him through the post, I had a quick word with Mary, who shook her head, and joined Keith at the bar.

Keith was just paying for the round. He left my pint beside me and carried the tray to our table. The blonde woman had a hot oven waiting and at my request she put a meat pie into it. I had experienced the local meat pies and they are good. The savoury smell soon made more mouths than mine water.

'One of those for me, Jane,' said a voice behind my right shoulder. It added, 'I'll be damned! Is that you, Ron?'

I looked round. The man in overalls was making for the door. Bruce Connerty was close by and looking at me in surprise. 'It must be years,' he said. 'What brings you here?' He was far from drunk but even his best friend, which I would never have claimed to be, could hardly have called him sober. His eyes were slightly out of focus and his tongue seemed to want to go its own way.

'Just passing,' I said. 'I fancied a pie and a pint.'

'My pint's on that table. Come and join me.'

'I'll bring your pies over in a minute,' the blonde woman said obligingly.

I paid her for both pies. It seemed best to go and sit with him rather than draw his attention to the company I was keeping. Looking back, I saw Ian glaring at me. Keith was already heading for the door.

Ian said later that he had made up his mind to get everybody out of there after one quick drink, but as soon as he saw Uncle Ron talking with the suspect he knew that his hand had been forced. He asked Keith to meet his reinforcements on their arrival in the village, bring them at least as far as the pub doorway and give him the nod.

He also gave some consideration to going into the church next door and praying, not least that my uncle might be struck down by pestilence or lightning, preferably both, but he decided that his presence in the bar might be urgently required.

Bruce did most of the talking, mostly because I couldn't think of anything that I could be sure Ian wouldn't tick me off for saying. Bruce was in a reminiscent mood but he'd had enough to drink that his memory was clouded. Several times he got muddled between capers he'd been up to in my company with mischief he'd made with some other boyhood crony.

It was quite a relief when Ian came to join us even if he was looking very stern. He pulled up a chair and sat down. 'You are Bruce Connerty?'

Bruce looked at him through narrowed eyes, sensing hostility. 'I am. Who the hell are you?'

Ian fumbled for the identification that he wasn't carrying. 'I am—'

At that moment the blonde woman arrived with our pies. She leaned across in front of Ian, cutting off his introduction, and fiddled with cutlery. At last she straightened up.

'I am Detec—'

Bruce was not listening. 'How much?' he asked the woman.

'Detective Insp—'

'They're paid,' she said.

Ian started again. 'My name is Fellowes and I am—'

Bruce still was not listening. 'You paid?' he asked me.

'—am a detective—'

'Yes.'

'—detective inspector—'

'You shouldn't have done that. How much were they?' Bruce fumbled in his pocket.

'Forget it,' I said. Now that we were here, I felt guilty, as if I owed him something for my betrayal. I had never really liked Bruce very much, just enough to share the occasional pint and talk about the football, and he was nothing special in the way of human beings, but I had never been a police nark and somehow the situation smacked of the Last Supper. To have taken his money would have reeked of thirty pieces of silver. Silly, but that's the way I felt at the time.

'Well, thanks.' Bruce Connerty forked up a slice of pie and filled his mouth. I was more cautious. I had been warned by seeing pies already in the oven when the blonde woman opened its door and I had felt the radiated heat from ten feet away.

Ian had his chance and he took it. 'I am Detective Inspector Fellowes of the Lothian and Borders Constabulary.'

Bruce had discovered for himself how hot was the pie. He couldn't chew, let alone swallow. He raised his eyebrows, blinked and made a helpless gesture. His expression was a mixture of pain and disbelief.

'I wish to speak to you about the death of Daniel Graham two years ago,' Ian said.

Bruce had begun to sweat and his eyes were watering. He made a faint whinnying sound. His feet tramped under the table and I noticed that the tip of his nose had turned white. He opened his mouth and breathed deeply and repeatedly until the bite of pie was cool enough to deal with. When at last he had managed to empty his mouth he held up his hand in a delaying gesture and took a pull at his beer. 'What the hell?' he managed to croak at last.

'You remember when Mr Graham fell to his death? It was the day your brother died in a car crash. Mr Graham wasn't found until the next day,' Ian added helpfully.

'I mind being told about it,' Bruce said.

'You didn't climb the hill above the quarry that day?'

Bruce's face took on a stubborn look. 'I didn't go near Gillespie House that day. And I've never climbed that hill in my life.'

'You've just been picked out,' Ian said, 'from among the men in this bar at the time, by a witness who saw you climbing the hill beside the quarry, almost on the heels of Mr Graham. That's the Mr

170

Graham who was in the process of losing a great deal of money in your brother's various dealings and wasn't any too pleased about it.'

'Your witness is mistaken,' Bruce said. 'Whoever he is. Or lying.' He took another, more cautious, mouthful of his pie and looked at me. His look was a silent question but I could not make out what he was asking – whether I was the witness or whether Ian was bluffing.

'I'm sorry, Bruce,' I said, 'but there's some evidence that says you did go up the hill.' I remembered something else and decided to take a chance. 'What's more, Dougie Slattery saw your car in the quarry when he did his runner.'

Bruce Connerty stayed calm. He sat in silence, working his way through his pie, which was now cool enough to eat. I copied him. The moment when an innocent man would have denied everything had passed. I could almost see the wheels turning in his head, balancing the flat denial against the possible benefit of making a slightly clean breast of it.

In the end, he sat back and looked Ian in the eye. 'I'll tell you how it was,' he said clearly.

'You don't have to say anything,' Ian said. 'Anything you do say will be written down and may be given in evidence.' He felt for his customary notebook and didn't find it. I gave him some scraps of paper and a stub of pencil.

'No, I'll tell you,' said Bruce. 'I nearly spilled it all at the time.' There was a hush in the bar. 'I was going in to see Nat, the back way, when I saw Mr Graham's car in the quarry. Nat had said to keep him away from the place – Mr Graham had been making a damn nuisance of himself, and there was

171

nothing he could say that made a damn bit of difference to anything.

'I'd never been up the hill before, that much was true. But you can see the top of the hill from the windows so I knew that from the hill you could get a good look at the house. And for all I knew he had a rifle with him. From what I'd heard, he was quite angry enough to knock Nat off if he could. He'd popped his cork whenever Nat's name was mentioned in company. So I followed him up.'

'And did he have a rifle?' Ian asked.

Bruce hesitated and I saw him arrange his face into an expression of guileless honesty. 'No. He'd no sort of weapon with him except a heavy walking stick.'

'There was no stick found,' Ian said sharply.

Bruce shrugged. 'It fell with him,' he said. 'It was nothing fancy. I dare say that nobody thought anything of one length of stick among the weeds. I told him that if he wanted to see any of his money again he'd do better to keep on Nat's good side, but anyway that he was on private property and to get down off the hill and go away. He swore at me and I told him more or less the same again but in different words, just trying to get the message home to him. Well, I thought I was telling the truth. I didn't know how bad things were, or that Nat was already dead.'

'How do you know that your brother was dead by then?' Ian demanded.

'Because I'd seen the police cars arriving as I climbed the hill,' Bruce said, with exaggerated patience. 'It didn't take long to figure out the timing once I heard what had been happening.'

172

'All right,' Ian said. 'Go on.'

Bruce nodded. 'I said that I'd give him laldie if he didn't get away home – not threatening, you understand, but just trying to make him take it in. Well, I wasn't going to hit him,' he said with a great air of virtue. 'I've been a club bouncer and I was Nat's debt collector and repo man. Repossession of cars on HP, you know? I've trained in martial arts. The courts go hard on a man like me if he gets violent, especially with an older man. And there's nearly always somebody sees you, out in the country. So I wasn't going to put a single mark on him. Well, you ask your witness and he'll tell you the same as I am.

'He stood there for a minute, just grinning at me. "Laldie?" he said. "You'll give me laldie? Like hell! I'll give you laldie and I'll kill you too." And then he came at me, swinging his stick so that it whistled, heavy though it was.

'I dived aside and rolled back to my feet and he came after me again and I dodged again and he was seeing red – literally, it wouldn't surprise me. And the third or fourth time I dodged out of the way, he ran clean off the edge. I heard him land with a thump but I wasn't going to look over the edge for myself, I'd've got vertigo and gone down the same way.'

'And,' Ian said, 'of course you didn't deliberately place yourself near the brink so that when he ran at you and you dodged he'd go over?'

'If that's what your witness says, he's dreaming,' Bruce said. He drained his pint. 'I went down and sat in my car for most of an hour. I thought that we must have been seen from the cottage and that your lot would turn up at any moment. Then I thought I'd call you in myself. But then I changed my mind. I couldn't bring him back. He'd fallen. What good would I do by involving myself? Damn all. It wouldn't change a thing except to let me in for a whole lot of hassle. You might have said that I'd pushed him over and I couldn't prove that I hadn't. What happens now?'

Ian nodded to Keith who went out. 'My officers will take you in to Newton Lauder to make a formal statement. It will be up to the procurator fiscal to decide whether you go before the sheriff there to answer charges.' Two uniformed constables came in and stood ready. 'Go with these men. I'll stay here and get the names of all these witnesses.' He turned to me. 'You lucky devils can go home and eat now.'

'Try the hot pies,' I said. 'They're good.'

Bruce got to his feet. 'Before I go,' he said to me, 'what was the other evidence that put me on the hill?'

'The keeper had been putting down wheat for the pheasants,' I said. 'That's what they like best. Nat must have been buying it in from a farmer on lower ground. You're too high up here for wheat to grow commercially; I could only see barley in the fields. But there were a few stalks of old wheat in the dug ground beside your front door, just about where somebody would brush himself down if he'd been rolling around and fighting in the straw,' I was playing the Great Detective. I was sure that everyone in the bar was impressed.

Bruce looked at me coldly. 'You bloody fool,' he said with feeling. 'I worked for a farmer near Coldstream through most of last summer. It'd be a

174

bloody miracle if I hadn't tracked some wheat grains home with me.'

Bruce could probably have retracted his admissions despite the number of witnesses to them. But he stuck to the story that he had told us. Frankly, nobody believed it but it was a very difficult story to disprove. The whole case was reopened, but in the end the procurator fiscal decided that there was little chance of a conviction and Bruce got away with it. He's kept his nose clean ever since, so no great harm was done.

And that's about all there is to the story. Except that Mrs Connerty's finances seemed to improve not long after. Perhaps she found a new boyfriend, although the neighbourhood saw no signs of fresh visitors. Anyway, she was able to hire some men to put the house back in order.

She also asked whether Mary wouldn't like to come back and work for her again. There were good staff quarters, if I came along too. But I explained that I had my own house just where I wanted to live and handy to most of my work. That left Mary to choose between me and her old employer. I've pointed out that my house is much the handier to a school, but it's taking her longer than I like to give an answer.

Mrs Connerty also gave me a letter to deliver to Dougie. I took it along, together with the passport, and caught him at home in his cellar. I made sure that he knew who was coming in. He was not a man that I'd willingly trust around firearms.

Dougie lit the lamp and read through the letter carefully, twice. Then he folded it up and put it in his pocket. 'She wants me to come back and work for her,' he said. 'Chauffeur, gardener and handyman. What do you think?'

'You're still wanted,' I pointed out.

'Nobody's watching for me very hard. Your niece's husband let everybody think I've gone abroad. The lady says she never sees anyone from the old days. There's neighbours, of course, but none within half a mile and she doesn't mix with them much. The nearest house changed hands last year.' Dougie looked at himself in the shard of mirror that stood on one of his rough shelves. He stroked his beard. 'My hair's greyer and my beard's come in mostly red. With these whiskers, who'd recognize me?'

'You're thinner and paler,' I said, 'and with hardly having heard another voice except the radio, you've lost some of your accent. If you keep it that way, very few would know you again.'

'And of those who might, I don't think there's one as would clype on me.'

'You'd need somewhere to have come from,' I pointed out. 'Nobody'd think twice if you were explained away as being somebody's cousin from Edinburgh or Dunfermline. Mine if you like,' I added.

He looked at me doubtfully. 'Maybe,' he said. 'But I don't know. I've got kind of used to being my own boss. What do you think yourself, Ron?'

'We're not getting any younger,' I said. 'What's going to happen when you need a doctor or a dentist?'

'You could be right,' he said. 'Thanks, Ronnie. Maybe it's time I came back to civilization. I could have me a dog again. Quits?'

176

I still owed him one for pushing me into the river, at some risk to my life, and there had been one or two other things. I took out the envelope that Mrs Connerty had given me and moved forward, placing myself between him and the shelf where his shotgun waited. 'You'd better have one of your passports,' I said. 'Then whatever you decide, you're equipped.' But as I handed it over, we fumbled it and it fell to the floor.

He bent to pick it up.

I took out and extended the radio aerial that I had been carrying in my pocket. The car wash had snapped it off somebody's car and I had retrieved it from the refuse bin for this very purpose. And I lashed him across the backside with it as hard as I could.

You should have been there to see him! He straightened up quicker than I'd have believed. His eyes opened until I could see the whites all the way round and I thought they'd pop out and dangle down his cheeks. And then he began to dance round and round in a circle, hissing through his teeth so hard that the fine spray seemed ready to produce a rainbow. When at last he came to a halt – but still tramping with his feet, like Bruce with a mouthful of scorching pie – and stopped holding himself for long enough to mop his watering eyes, I spoke to him.

'Now, Dougie,' I said. 'Now we're quits.'

The typescript has come back to me after copy-editing and the publisher has asked me to update the story and to add a few words of explanation, which will at least enable me to while away a few more hours of this seemingly endless pregnancy. If these notes should break off abruptly the reader may guess that my ordeal is ending at last.

According to Ian, the local solicitor, who as well as being an old friend is a crafty old so-and-so, advised Bruce to stick firmly to his story, risking a manslaughter verdict rather than one of murder. His advice seems to have been good, in hindsight – but perhaps the definition of the intelligent person is that he can anticipate what we other mortals can only see in retrospect.

Another definition might be that he can solve problems by observation and lateral thinking. At this, my father excels. So when I began to worry, I phoned, asking him to come in and visit me while Ian was out of the house. Dad arrived within half an hour.

'What can you possibly want to say to your own father that you couldn't say in front of your husband?' he asked me. 'Do you have some ghastly secret? Are you afraid that my first grandchild will be black?'

'Don't be an ass,' I told him. 'Where could I find a black lover around here? No, it's about Mrs Connerty and her new-found wealth.'

'Would you call it wealth?' he asked with apparent casualness.

'Compared to what she was managing on before,' I said, 'it's the height of affluence. I was sorry for the woman. I liked her and I know that she was once something special in your life. But if she's found her late husband's little hoard, that money really belongs to all the people he stole it from.'

Dad pointed his finger at me like a pistol. 'That's where you're wrong, Cleverclogs. Nat was propping up his business by means of loans from the banks and the banks insisted on his obtaining what they call *Bonds of Caution* from an insurance company. They never made a song about it for fear of starting a landslide and making their own investors nervous, but in the end the insurance company paid out. It didn't cover everything, but most creditors recovered a good three-quarters of what they'd lost or invested.'

In turn, I pointed my finger at him. 'Aha!' I said. 'Then the money belongs to the insurance company.'

'What money was recovered has been handed over to the insurance company, every damn penny of it, so put that in your sanctimonious pipe and smoke it.' I thought for a moment that he was going to put his tongue out at me as he used to do when I was a child caught in error, but he refrained. 'They had been offering the usual reward of ten per cent and that's what the widow has been lavishing on her property. Of course, you must remember that it was ten per cent of a very large sum. So it certainly has made the widow's life a little easier.'

'Just as I thought,' I said. 'You do know more about it than the rest of us. Does Ian know?'

'You can't expect me to tell you that,' Dad said.

'He'd have to,' I decided. 'And he didn't tell me. Just wait until he comes home.'

'You can't blame your husband for being discreet about his work.'

'Yes, I can. Now we're getting to the truth. The only reason I can see why he wouldn't tell me about it would be that there was something you didn't want Mum to know.'

'Like what?' he demanded indignantly.

My brain was catching up with my tongue. 'Like

you found the money, which is what I suspected all along. You could have claimed the reward for yourself,' I said triumphantly, 'and you kicked it back to your old girlfriend.'

Dad looked quickly around the room, in case Mum was lurking in a corner. 'Don't tell me that you're looking for a cut—'

'I'm not going to tell you any such thing,' I said indignantly. 'You didn't bring me up to be a blackmailer. But if you don't tell me where it was and how you came to find it, I'll tell Mum.'

'And you say you're not a blackmailer! Very well, this once I'll pay you off. It was very simple. If you've edited the whole of Ronnie's scribble you must know most of it by now. You remember what Nat called up to his wife before he drove off?'

'The most anybody seemed to be fairly sure of was the word "castle",' I said.

'Perhaps. Did Ronnie mention the slab in the garden?'

'In the lawn?'

'As it turned out, it wasn't in the lawn but in one of the borders, not that it matters.'

'He mentioned it in passing,' I said. 'According to him, there seemed to be the outline of a couple of babies on it.'

'Try the Heavenly Twins,' said Dad. 'And remember what Nat named his dogs.'

'Castor and Pollux!' I exclaimed. 'So what Nat was saying was that the money was under the gravestone of his favourite dog!' But I was still not satisfied. 'Dad, can you look me in the eye and tell me that the insurance company got its ninety per cent of every cent under the gravestone?'

He looked me in the eye and gave me that assurance, but I remain unconvinced. The money that the widow must have at her disposal seems to me to be more than ten per cent of the sort of sum I could imagine Nat Connerty being able to lay aside in cash.

When Ian came home that night, I sat him down with a drink and opened him up like a can of beans. (Memo to husbands: Ve haf vays of making you talk!) Then I let him grovel for some minutes in apology for having kept me in the dark over the recovery of Nat Connerty's hoard. With the proper mood once established, I moved on towards what I really wanted to know.

'Just how satisfied were you with Bruce Connerty's story?' I asked him.

Ian seemed to accept that the time for reticence was past. 'On a scale of one to ten, about six. There can be a very fine line between accident and manslaughter, but it's a line that the law has to draw over and over again. The procurator fiscal said that we couldn't disprove the story, so that was enough.'

'You don't sound too worried about it,' I said. 'Did you believe him when he quoted Dan Graham as saying "I'll kill you too"?'

Ian saw where I was heading and he tried to duck. 'In the context—'

'Don't give me contexts,' I said. 'According to Bruce Connerty, Mr Graham was grinning when he said, "I'll kill you too." To me, that doesn't mean "I'll kill you as well as beating you up." Come on, give. He killed Nat Connerty, didn't he? You know I'll get it out of you in the end.'

Ian sighed and looked longingly out of the window.

'Are you sure you don't want a job in the police?' he asked me. 'You'd be a whizz in the interrogation room.' He pretended to cower away from me. 'No, no, please don't hit me again.'

I refused to laugh. 'What do you know that I don't?' I asked him.

'Not a great deal,' he admitted. 'But some. Looking through the files, I saw that some thorough busybody on the scene of Daniel Graham's fall had made a meticulous list of the contents of his pockets and of his car and put them on file. That prompted me to ask a few questions of a friendly pathologist.

'It doesn't seem that the car could have been got at. So the only way that Nat Connerty's smash could have been other than accidental or suicidal would have been if he had been drugged or poisoned shortly before.

'Graham had given Connerty a cigar, which seemed out of key for a man in a high state of indignation. Ronnie tells me that Connerty was seen lighting the cigar as he halted at his gate. Graham couldn't have known that Connerty would choose that moment to light up. Graham was watching from the hill. Perhaps he was waiting for Connerty to collapse, dead or unconscious, so that he could both work off his venom and take advantage of the confusion and the rush to hospital to give the house another search. Was there anything, I asked my friendly pathologist, that could have been injected into the cigar that would have brought on unconsciousness or death?

'My friend's first thought was of cyanide. But I had got my hands on the original pathologist's report. Blood samples had been taken and they had been

182

tested for cyanide, to determine whether death had occurred before or during the fire, because cyanide is often present in smoke. There was no cyanide in the blood but there was soot in the lungs, confirming that Nat Connerty was still breathing when the fire started.

'His second suggestion was nicotine. It happens that the laboratory has a policy of keeping blood samples for three years, in case of subsequent litigation or allegations of negligence. I asked for Connerty's sample to be tested for nicotine and it came up positive.'

'But he was smoking a cigar,' I pointed out.

'Quite so. They couldn't tell me whether the nicotine had been a lethal dose. Three of four drops of the pure alkaloid will kill, or a teaspoonful of the insecticide. Looking back through the records, I see that the pathologist who gave evidence at the Fatal Accident Inquiry mentioned traces of nicotine, but it was assumed to be derived from one of the cigars Connerty was known to enjoy and the local rag didn't even bother to mention it. My pathological pal suggested that when the cigar reached a point laced with nicotine alkaloid, Nat Connerty would have blacked out immediately before more than a trace had entered his bloodstream. If he was still breathing when the car caught fire, a lungful of smoke and flames would have almost obliterated the traces in his lungs and, of course, the cigar was totally destroyed.

'Graham's business was agricultural chemicals. He had an assortment of samples in his car, including the pure alkaloid of nicotine which seems a strange substance to be carried as a sample, plus a whole range of syringes down to the very smallest. Presum-

183

ably Daniel Graham didn't expect to die before he could dispose of them. They went back to his widow along with the car, but the officer who made the notes assured me that the smallest of the syringes would have been quite suitable for introducing a liquid into a cigar.'

'Would it have acted so quickly?' I asked. 'Nat Connerty only got a few miles down the road.'

'The wonder is that he got as far as he did,' Ian said. 'The symptoms would include sudden collapse followed by respiratory paralysis. I can only think that the injection of nicotine was placed half an inch down the cigar. The moment the burning tip reached that point and he took another puff, Nat Connerty was as good as dead.'

Ian was rapidly convincing me but it was strange that there had been no burst of activity, with exhumations and hearings before the sheriff. 'You've kept very quiet about all this,' I said.

Ian shrugged and helped himself to a second drink. 'Why rock the boat?' he asked. 'There's been no miscarriage of justice but quite the reverse.'

'What is the reverse?' I asked curiously. 'A carriage of justice?'

Ian shrugged again, not to be diverted by semantics. 'I'm satisfied that Nat Connerty was murdered by Daniel Graham. Daniel Graham died immediately afterwards, possibly by accident but more probably at the hands of the dead man's brother. We'll never know for sure which. If the case had been officially reopened, that would have been the version of events that I'd have put forward. But justice has already been adequately served. I believe that the sheriff's two verdicts of Accident and Suicide might well have read Murder and Accident. I also believe that Graham's widow knew nothing about her husband's crime but, again, either way it could never be proved. I can't see that anything would be gained by reopening either case, except a lot of hassle and heartbreak for everybody and some profitless work for the police, the procurator fiscal's office and the courts.'

'And a lot of profit for the lawyers,' I pointed out.

'That's another reason,' Ian said grimly. He has never quite come to terms with the logic of expensively prosecuting somebody for an offence of which they are obviously guilty and then stumping up further large sums in Legal Aid for lawyers to pick technical loopholes in the case. In his view Justice is perfect, the Law must be accepted with all its faults but the Legal Machine is a dangerously antiquated and creaking vehicle for transporting the other two.

And that is just about the end of our story, all but the part relating to Mary Jablinska, my Uncle Ron and Mrs Connerty's hope of getting Mary back to work for her.

The outcome

Sorry. Got to go.